ONE TRICKED PHONEY

One Tricked Phoney

Byron James-Adams

Thanks again to my beta readers. Vic, Mel & Lil.
Cover Art: Canva by author.
Internal Book Design: Ingram Sparks.

Nic Thorn and his associates investigate frauds, scams and genuine misunderstandings. These modern-day adventures lead them from one lively caper to another, this time involving a portrait provenance, an invoice inaccuracy, and a recycler's relapse, on their travels from Brisbane, Adelaide and across to the South Australian border.

One Tricked Phoney is the first book in the Nic Thorn & Associates Investigations series by Byron James-Adams. A version of the story was released in November 2020, under the title "One Jaded Rose." It has been revised and republished here to align with the series of books available within the Ingram Sparks catalogue. Other titles include Two Hurtled Gloves, Three French Bens, Four Brooding Birds, Five Mouldy Bins, Six Geezers Lying, Seven Hapless Hoops, Eight Dave's Are Weak, Nine Means Know and Ten Little Idioms.

CHAPTER 1

Rosemary Palmer was standing on the wrap-around balcony of her Queenslander in the leafy high-end Brisbane suburb of Hamilton. She heard it before she saw it, the growling throb of a Ford Mustang crawling down her street. Oh, please don't let it be him she thought, she needed her +1 to be quiet and conservative, but her hopes were dashed as it came to a slow stop outside her home.

Damn...

The driver seemed to be taking an extraordinarily long time to exit the car and the darkened windows made it even more difficult to catch a glimpse of him. Finally, he went, but didn't look up to where she was standing, he walked around to the car's boot and extracted a bouquet of Lisianthus. *At least he has read my Vita Brevis dating profile* she thought, as she watched him walk to the front gate.

Giving him the once over from her makeshift citadel, she was initially satisfied that the handsome dark-haired man dressed in the standard 'Australian cocky' attire might just do at such short notice.

She guessed him to be mid-thirties, one point nine metres tall, around one hundred and ten kilograms, and he wore the chinos, RM's, blue twill shirt and checked wool blazer rather well, maybe too well. He struggled with the flower arrangement, front gate and intercom system, so Rose called out to get his attention, and he looked up at her.

He smiled. Did his eyes just sparkle? Maybe he was just squinting into the sun. Yes, that was it, he was squinting into the sun.

'Are you Rose?' he called out as he waited patiently at the gate for her to arrive. When she opened the gate and he stepped through, he said 'Nice,' but she didn't know if he was referring to her sprawling Hamilton home, or if it was directed at her. He introduced himself. 'Nic Thorn. Nice to meet you. This house is nice. Have you been here long?'

'It's my family home, well it's owned by the Family Trust and all that stuff, but I do stay here and look after it when my folks are away. Otherwise, Mr and Mrs Croud, the live-in gardener and housekeeper, are always here. My parents will be back later this afternoon from their trip down to the Gold Coast. They were checking out...' Rose stopped mid-sentence realising that he didn't need to know any of that, as she only needed to know if he was free for this afternoon's +1 event.

Nic smiled. 'You're dating profile doesn't match your...well, it doesn't do you justice, Rose.'

Rose looked at him wondering if that was a good or bad thing.

Nic continued; 'So, tell me about these +1 things. Wedding, engagement, drinks at work? Am I getting warmer?'

'Well no, actually, I need you to come with me to a funeral, then the wake, and then a will reading. It will be interesting, to say the least. He was a good friend and a true gentleman.'

'OK, I haven't been on a date to that type of thing before. It could make for a curious outing.'

'It's not a date, it's a job. You're my +1 for the afternoon that's all,' she clarified quickly, then led him through the extensive front garden, into the extensive house, and they stopped in the extensive kitchen, where the Housekeeper was attending to the extensive morning chores.

They sat at the kitchen table and Rose crossed her arms over her chest. 'Sorry Mr Thorn, I'm a bit nervous about all of this dating stuff, and I tend to talk too much when I get nervous. Coffee, tea...what would you like? Mrs Croud will get that for you and tell me more about yourself. What do you do, and why are *you* using the Vita Brevis dating app?'

'Chai Tea if you have it, and yep will do, but first I need to find a vase for these.' He stood, then proceeded to open kitchen cabinets looking for a suitable receptacle for the flowers.

He couldn't find anything suitable, so sat down.

'You're very confident aren't you, Mr Thorn? Just put them in the sink and Mrs Croud will deal with them later. I need to find out what, if any, skeletons you may have in your closet - or personality traits that I need to be aware of - if you are going to spend the afternoon with me and my family. Do you live in Brisbane? Do you work? Are you married?'

'Well, confidence is my middle name, so you didn't read my Vita Brevis profile at all did you?' he replied, then added; 'Yes, Yes and No. All good questions though. Firstly, I am living in Brisbane at the moment as I have an apartment in Southbank. Do I work?.... Well, that is complicated. I like Vita Brevis for the pictures and to know my competition. Sorry, what was the other question?'

'Are you married?' Nic appeared to stammer with the response. 'Well ... no.'

Rose wondered why he had hesitated with that response, but let it go for the moment. Nic continued. 'So what time does this shindig start then? I'm happy to be your white knight on a steed if it suits.'

Rose rolled her eyes. 'You don't have a suit of armour, a steed or a horse.'

'A steed *is* a horse, but I have a white pony – the Mustang out the front has all the horsepower I'll ever need.'

Good grief...

Nic proceeded to explain his complicated work situation. 'Well, I buy stuff, sell stuff, find stuff, lose stuff, and do stuff. So, tell me a little more about yourself, Rose. I don't know, do you hold a grudge or anything like that?'

Rose sighed. 'Well, my father says that I am immature, and I hold resentment toward my mother, in fact, I don't like being around them much at all.'

'Whoa, OK, duly noted. Do you work?'

Rose took a breath. 'At the moment, no. I did have a part share in a retail couture and coffee shop outlet, but that closed down when they did the upgrade along Kingsford Smith Drive, at Brett's Wharf. It was called 'The She Shed'. We decided to shut down for a while instead of relocating until we decide where to go next.'

'We? We who?'

'My Uncle Albert's niece Sandy, and me. It's his funeral that we're going to this afternoon if you can make it. Part of his money was in the shop, but it is all gone now. The banks took it back.'

'All banks are bastards, and all men too.' Nic commented quietly whilst sipping on his tea.

Rose sighed again. 'Right then, if you're good to do this, can you pick me up around three as the funeral starts at four, the wake is straight afterwards. It's in the same place. Then we'll have to do a short walk down Eagle Street to the lawyer's office at Riparian Plaza, for the will reading.'

'Where's the funeral service? In the city?'

'Yes, at the Marriott Hotel. Don't ask how Uncle

Albert managed that. He always was a bit eccentric. I assume the cost is all coming out of his estate, what's left of it anyway.'

'OK, that suits me fine. I'll rearrange a couple of things but will pick you up here just before three. I have to make a drop off in the city myself, so that will work.'

Rose looked at him pondering about arriving in the Mustang together. 'Can you pick me up in something a little less, you know, showy? Do you have another car?'

Nic nodded. 'Sure do, and that's one of the things I'll need to change. The other car I have at the moment is about seventy years old and may not be as comfortable as the Mustang.'

Nic finished his tea, hand washed the cup out in the sink, wiped it dry, put it in the cupboard, pulled the existing arrangement of flowers from the vase on the table, replaced them with the Lisianthus, fussed with them a little, showed himself out, and left her there standing alone in the kitchen.

Who was that man of mystery, and where was the mild-mannered 'Clark Kent' type, she needed as her +1 instead?

Rose was again standing on the balcony waiting. It was just before 3 p.m., and she thought that Nic wasn't going to turn up. A mid-fifties silver Mercedes 300SL came slowly down the street. She knew something about cars as her father had a small selection stored underneath the house, and speculated it had to be worth over a million dollars. The car stopped out the front of her place, the gull-wing door opened and Nic climbed out. He was dressed all in black, and she assumed it was Armani, and she wondered who wears Armani to a funeral.

'Nice', he commented looking up at her. Rose felt it was to her that he was referring to this time and called out to him. 'I asked for something less showy, Mr Thorn, and that is not less showy.'

Nic called back. 'It is over seventy years old, Miss Palmer. The doors don't work properly, the windows don't quite shut and it's a four-speed manual. You said something less showy than the Mustang. This is it.'

Rose came through the front gate, to review the classic car, and Nic asked her to do a twirl in her pale blue and pink chiffon dress, but she realised he was admiring the car more than her, as he began to take photos of it with his phone. 'Is it yours, Mr Thorn?'

'Not quite, but please call me Nic, and may I call you Rose? Jump in and I will explain on the way. I did have to fix it up a little bit though, along with a few changes here and there.'

Rose carefully stepped in and waited for more of an explanation, but he only responded with, 'It's not mine, but I know how much this one sold for.' Not wanting to pursue it any further, she started to explain why she needed a +1 for Uncle Albert's funeral. 'My family are a little different, Nic. We are Palmers.'

Nic looked over at her. 'Whoa – as in the Palmers?'

'No, well, not exactly *The* Palmers of Queensland, but still Palmers after all. Maybe somewhere distantly there could be a crossover, but I've never bothered to find out. My parents made their money, not just inherited it. I mean they're not in the top echelon of Brisbane society, but sometimes we do get to breathe the rarefied air.'

Rose stopped talking, closed her eyes and enjoyed the drive in the classic Mercedes. It was over all too soon though as they had reached their destination having just come through the Valley. They had missed the Marriott Hotel turn-off and were a little further down Eagle Street when she saw a man standing in the middle of the traffic.

'What's he waiting for? What a stupid place to stand.'

Nic stopped the car against the kerb. 'Actually, he's waiting for me to deliver this car to him.'

Rose knew it to be a "No Standing Zone".

Nic continued: 'We have to go into the Bank to do the payment transfer, so would you mind staying in the car until we come back? If a brown bomber comes along just do your best to convince him that you don't know anything about it, and are just waiting for help. You know, the old damsel in distress trick, and dressed like that I don't think you will have any trouble convincing him.'

'What if the parking inspector is a her?'

'I'm sure you'll manage, trust me. I would get out of the car anyway.'

Nic bounded down to meet with the prospective buyer/owner, whatever the anxious-looking man was, and Rose considered she would be anxious too if she saw her newly purchased million-dollar car driven through Brisbane city traffic.

Brushing down the light chiffon dress trying to take the creases out, Rose allowed herself to feel pretty, after all, being able to buy off the rack was easier when you still had your youthful shape and access to couture stock at wholesale prices.

Rose was miles away in thought when someone rapped softly on the car window, and pulling herself out of the reverie, looked at who was intruding. It was a parking inspector, and as they were still parked on a yellow line in Eagle Street, knew she was in trouble.

Rose cursed softly. 'Damn you Nic,' and smiled at the man, but upon second look she decided it might be a woman, then attempted to open the gullwing door, but realised she didn't know how. Rose raised her palms with a defeated gesture, but the man/woman waited for her to step out of the car.

Rose cursed again. 'Damn it Nic, where are you?'

Finally, Nic was coming towards her. He was all smiles and chummy with the new owner, and Rose realised he may not be aware of the dilemma with the parking inspector, so she pressed on the horn - it sounded like a soft whine, instead of the musical, E-flat note, that the pre-1960s Mercedes are renowned for. Nic looked up, jogged up to the car and let her out, all the while maintaining his composure.

Rose stepped from the car and nodded to the parking inspector, trying to explain that she didn't know how to get the door open, but was being ignored.

Nic took complete control of the situation, and in three slick movements, handed the new owner the keys, stopped the traffic to allow his departure, and turned back to the inspector.

All in less than 60 seconds.

Nic held out his hand to the inspector and placed his other hand on her shoulder. Rose thought it was very assuming of him to take this approach, but it seemed to be working. Soon they were both smiling and with a polite thanks, Nic mentioned something about dobbing in the real parking abusers.

The inspector began to move away, and Rose realised it might be an opportune time to again offer an apology, but the woman just sneered at her.

CHAPTER 2

Rose and Nic watched the Parking Inspector saunter down the road, then turned to make the short walk up the road to the Marriott. The whole car swap/parking fiasco had taken no more than twenty minutes, and Rose was happy they would still be one of the first to arrive.

They entered the Marriott Hotel foyer, and Nic nodded to an easel displaying a headshot of Albert, along with the directive to the first floor. 'Gee Rose, I didn't realise Albert was such a good-looking man.' The photograph was of a man in his early forties, wearing a leather flight cap and goggles as if he were a seasoned pilot.

Rose shrugged her shoulders. 'The picture is at least thirty years old Nic, and most likely the headwear has been added in later with Photoshop.'

'You are one jaded Rose, aren't you?'

Rose looked up at him as they ascended the stairs to the first floor. 'Wait until the theatrical show at the funeral, then the wake, then all the fanfare at the reading. You'll see what I have to put up with.'

Nic grinned. 'I can't wait. Can we please go in now though? I'm so looking forward to it, sounds exciting.'

There was a table off to the right of the double doors that led into where the ceremony would be, and it was covered in numerous name tags. Nic did a rough count. 'Expecting a big crowd, Rose?'

'Nope, that was just Uncle Albert. It will be his way to show how many people he knew, but the truth is that he was a lonely old man with time on his hands.'

They were each given a flute of champagne by one of the wait staff. Nic took a sip; 'This is Dom Perignon. I do prefer Bollinger.'

Rose decided not to drink it, returned her flute to the table, and asked for a sparkling mineral water instead, then proceeded to look for her name. Nic found it first and offered to pin it on her. She declined with a sharp slap of his hand but managed to jab herself in her finger while pinning it on herself - a tiny spot of blood appeared on the tip. Nic noticed and offered to lick the blood spot. Rose slapped his hand away. 'Behave yourself, Nic'.

'That's not in my nature, Rose.'

Nic was reviewing the names on the table and was surprised he recognised many of them. There were quite some high-profile invitees including Anna Bligh, David Campbell, Sir Malcolm Campbell, and George Costanza. There were also a couple of Hemsworths, Danny Kaye, Danni Minogue, Kylie Minogue, Campbell Newman, Sam Newman, and Alfred E Neumann, but he suddenly stopped when he got to the "T"s. He looked at the name label and read it again. It was a name he knew should not have been there, so he quickly collected it and dropped it into his pocket.

One pair of names stood out as they were from the Brisbane Gallery Of Modern Art, and Nic wondered what connection Albert had with GOMA. He was due to meet with them himself.

Nic softly nudged his shoulder into Rose. 'There are a lot of Palmers here too aren't there? Will my name be here somewhere? Or your Uncle Clive's?' Rose looked at him, picked up a label and slapped it to his chest. Taking it from her, read aloud, 'Oh, +1....how original.' Nic asked the hostess if she could provide a label with his actual name on it. She looked at Rose, who nodded her permission.

'Just put "Nic", but can you add the +1 on it too, please.'

Although early, they were allowed into the make-shift funeral parlour. Nic opened the doors and they stepped into a room that was set up like a Bedouin Tent. He looked around the colourful space and saw the line of belly dancers up on the stage. There were at least fifteen of them, so he indicated to Rose that they should sit somewhere near the front.

She declined.

They ended up in the middle of the seating area, and it wasn't long before the rest of the guests arrived. Nic was eager to find out who everyone was, so he kept probing Rose for a response, but she kept staring forward. He realised she was staring at the line of belly dancers who were now starting up their routine.

'If I kept staring at those scantily clad women like you are, I would get arrested, and what's with the casket up on the stage? It might get knocked over with all of those dancers jiggling around it.'

Rose sighed. 'It's only a small one, and looks secured.'

Nic nodded. 'OK, but what about it being only one and a half metres long? Uncle Albert looked much taller in the portrait downstairs.'

'It's empty Nic. Albert was cremated two days ago.'

Rose turned away to watch the throng of people making their way into the room. Nic leaned closer. 'Mm, do you know many of these people coming in then?'

'No, they are most likely from "Rent-a-Crowd." Have you heard of it?'

'Actually yes. I use them from time to time myself.' Nic was wondering why no one was greeting them but was relieved when a pretty young woman approached them - she was about Rose's age.

Rose leaned into him. 'This is Sandy. Be nice.'

Nic stood up and lightly kissed her hand when she offered it. 'Sorry to hear about Uncle Albert and 'The She Shed' too, Sandy. It was making a good turnover and showed good profits until the road re-routing closed you down.'

Sandy looked at Nic trying to work out who he was. 'I'm Nic, Rose's +1. Nice to meet you.' Rose, meantime, stood up from her chair. They hugged and she offered Sandy the seat next to her, then leaned into Nic. 'How do you know about the performance of our business?'

Nic smiled. 'Oh, didn't I mention that earlier, Rose? I also know stuff, find stuff and forget stuff too.'

Sandy placed her hand on Rose's knee and gave it a little squeeze. 'Albert was good to us you know. I'm interested to know what's going to happen to us now.'

Rose was softly smiling, but suddenly her expression changed to a look of concern. Nic noticed. 'So, who have you just spotted?'

Rose sighed. 'See the man that just came in with the two little girls and the very pretty woman?'

'Yes, who is he?'

'My ex-husband.'

Sandy had seen him now too. 'Michael is here too. I wonder why? And he's brought Dimond and the girls too.'

Nic joined the conversation. 'Did you say her name is Diamond?'

'Yes, Dimond without the 'a'. I went to St Margaret's at Clayfield with her. She was in the year below me at school.' Nic leaned forward. 'Tell me all about Michael then? How long were you married?'

'Well, I was only nineteen. Still at Uni. We got married.'

'Medical reasons?'

Sandy looked at him. 'Don't be nasty, Nic. It was annulled soon after.'

'So why then?'

Rose ignored the question, so Sandy took over. 'Rose's father needed to finalise a company merger, but it was going to roll over, it was a dead duck. So, he offered up his only daughter to get it over the line. They got married, but it was never supposed to be. Michael is a creep.'

Rose finally spoke. 'And he still thinks that I am interested in him. He keeps trying to contact me; via Tinder, and Linked-In, and inappropriately turning up at events, like Uncle Albert's funeral. The marriage was never even......."

'Consummated?' Nic inquired quietly.

'No Nic, I was never going to say that. The deal that my Father put together had already fallen over. I was just the sacrificial lamb. I've hated them for years, which is why I find...' Rose had stopped in mid-sentence as Nic stood up and made his way towards Michael and his little family. Sandy didn't make any effort to stop him.

They watched as Nic and Michael introduced themselves and to the children and Dimond. Nic then subtly guided Michael away from his little family group, and it was obvious from the body language that the conversation was no longer civil, and they took a selfie.

Sandy and Rose watched as Nic nodded towards them, and then they saw Michael look up towards them, then over to his children and wife. Michael's eyes dropped down, and then Nic returned.

Rose looked at him sternly. 'Just what did you say to him? You don't have to fight my battles. It was over ten years ago. I am so over him, and over it...and, and...you took a selfie.'

'Well, I pointed out to Michael that certain people can find out certain things about certain places that certain men frequent, that only take cash, and those places have certain rooms in the back for doing certain things with ladies who are not their spouses. He seemed to lose interest in pursuing you after hearing that.'

'How did you know he does all that?'

Nic shrugged. 'I didn't, but the look on his face when I reminded him about how much family matters, triggered something as he realised the errors of his ways. I did mention I know the owner of a certain XXX club at Petrie Terrace, I knew then I was close to the mark. He shouldn't bother you anymore.'

Sandy looked over at Michael. 'Look at that he's leaving, but Dimond and the girls are staying.' Sandy then excused herself, stood up, and moved off to talk with some of the others.

Nic leaned toward Rose. 'You should have warned me, Rose. I almost burst into laughter when he introduced the girls. Skye and Lucy, and his wife's name's Dimond. That's ridiculous.'

'Why?'

Nic was taken aback. 'The Beatles; the sixties, the song; Lucy in the Sky with Diamonds.'

'Nope, doesn't mean anything to me.'

'The Beatles, or the song?'

'I have heard of most of the bands from the sixties; The Beatles, The Animals, The Crickets, The Monkees and the band named after the owls.'

'Who?'

'That's them, The Who. I wasn't allowed to listen to music growing up. The Beatles, are they the men from Manchester?'

Nic shook his head. 'Manchester? No, that was Oasis, about forty years later. The Beatles were from Liverpool.'

Rose nodded. 'Although, I do like Frank Sinatra, Bing Crosby, Johnny Mathis, Kenny G, and that sort of music style. Oh, and there's that red-headed guy from England I like too. He got married recently I think.'

Nic smiled. 'Prince Harry?'

'Yep, that's him. He played that Wembley gig all by himself. Good on him.'

CHAPTER 3

They watched a man dressed as a sheik cross the stage in front of the line of dancers and stand at the podium until the music quietened. He took a microphone from a stage attendant and shuffled his notes in readiness to start. 'Good afternoon and thank you all for coming. Let me introduce myself. I am the Sheik and will be your emcee today. You might be wondering why Albert arranged all of this. He wasn't known as having Arabian influences, but it was mainly because he thought everyone, he knew was too intense. So that is why he arranged his last goodbye, *in-tents*.'

There was a small murmur of laughter and the emcee continued: 'Now, about Albert. Andrew Albert Adams, Bryan Albertus Brown, Campbell Bert Campbell.'

Nic whispered to Rose. 'Is there a Peter Al Palmer too? I thought you said he wasn't related.' Rose shook her head. 'He's not but wait for the next name. It's a doozy.' The sheik continued: 'Freddie Albert Flintstone. I think I will stop there though, as everyone knew him as Uncle Albert, but he wasn't anyone's uncle now was he?'

Nic looked at Rose and whispered again. 'I thought you said Sandy was his niece.'

'Sshh, let him speak.'

The sheik cleared his throat, neighed like a horse and began again: 'Albert had prepared a speech for me. He knew he was *dying* to get someone to read it, so here goes.' The sheik then proceeded to tell about all the exploits and expeditions around the world that Albert had been on, all the challenges and adversity he had faced, and how he had managed to cope with it all so well. He finished this reading with 'Such a hero Uncle Albert was, Ladies and Gentleman.'

The Rent-A-Crowd meantime was Oohing and Aaahing, while Rose slowly shook her head from side to side.

Nic whispered. 'What?'

Rose sighed. 'He never left Brisbane.'

The sheik paused to compose himself, took a deep breath, reached down to a folder next to the lectern, picked it up, and flicked through it. He then commented how much more he was obliged to read out today, but before he could restart the double doors swung open, and a man riding a small camel came in. The sheik stopped mid-paper shuffle and called out: 'We're so sorry Uncle Albert,' then he stormed off the stage. Nic whispered. 'Well, he was a post-Beatles fan then. Paul, the lovely Linda, and his band "Wings." Nic then looked toward the new intrusion. 'And who is that on the camel?'

Rose sighed. 'It's my Father.'

The camel was being led by two men, and there was a woman in tow carrying a large woven basket. She was walking submissively as if it were her role to collect any 'mistakes' made by the camel during the performance and proceeded to flick the contents from the basket. Small brown lumps were strewn through the air.

One of them landed next to Nic, he picked it up, looked at it and took a bite. 'It's a brownie, how appropriate.' Nic's gaze then went to the peasant woman.

Rose whispered: 'And she .... is my mother'.

The woman reached the stage, turned the basket upside down and spilt the remainder of the contents onto the floor into a small brown pile, then curtseyed and took a seat next to the stage.

'Do you know the two men too, Rose?'

'Yes, they both work with my father. I think one is called Steve and the other Stephen, but I never know which is which.'

The two men waited at the vacated space in front of the stage. The rider then rolled off the camel and one of the hosts led the camel back out through the doors. Nic grinned. 'Mm, midnight at the oasis? Put your camel to bed?'

Rose leaned forward. 'What's that Nic?'

'Oh, never mind.'

The new group had now made their way onto the stage, and Rose's Father stepped up to the lectern.

'Hello everybody. I am a Sheik and you may address my two colleagues as Stephen. You may call us "Sheik-n-Stephens.'

Nic groaned. 'That's bad, Rose.'

Rose responded with. 'I don't get it?'

'Shakin' Stephens, the Welsh singer from the eighties. "Behind the Green Door, This Old House", I can't think of any others at the moment though. He was a big hit way back when.'

'Oh, OK, and nope. Not heard of him. I was born in ninety-one.'

Nic shook his head. 'I have to get you into more music don't I?'

'I played music when I was at school.'

Nic smiled. 'Let me guess....Flute? Clarinet? Nope, something a little more stylish. The Oboe?'

'It was the xylophone. I was good at it too until Mark Teague decided he could pull the knobs off the ends of the batons, and use them as back scratchers.'

They listened to Rose's father read from his prepared notes and stumbled his way through more of Albert's adventures: The story had left Europe and was now somewhere in India. His two henchmen started to dance, gyrating around the floor space, doing the worm and generally an embarrassing show for grown men dressed in white bed sheets. Everybody else was cheering them on. They suddenly stopped, and Rose's father threw the rest of his readings into the air, and they scurried from the stage.

Another sheik quickly took his place, although this one was alone, he had two baskets with him. Nic clapped. 'What's next? This is a hoot, Rose.'

The new sheik started juggling bread rolls, one, two, three, four and it was impressive, then he added items from the second basket. These appeared to be jingling baby toys, and they were being spun in the air now too.

Nic whispered to Rose. 'I don't quite get it.'

Rose sighed. 'I think it's supposed to be "Sheik-rattle-and-roll."' Nic nodded. 'You're good at this, aren't you? Enjoying yourself yet?'

Rose looked at him and shook her head sideways, then Nic took another bite of the brownie and offered her some. She declined.

This latest sheik stopped his performance by throwing the rolls as far as he could into the room, and the music started up again, and then the belly dancers started a conga line. 'This is getting silly.' Rose remarked as they joined at the back of the line.

It left the room, snaking its way downstairs to the Marriot's dining area, then petered out in the foyer. The 'Rent a Crowd' people moved away as they were no longer required. Rose sighed and sat down. 'That was forty-five minutes of my life I won't get back again.' Nic was still swaying with the beat, then sat down too.

A small area had been cordoned off so everyone that remained had designated seats. Nic calculated that there were only about twenty people left including Sandy, Rose's parents, the two Stephens and the couple from GOMA. Those that needed to be redressed into normal business attire and the discarded bedsheets were quickly collected.

Nic looked around and noticed Dimond and her girls had come down too, but Michael was still nowhere to be seen. 'Can I meet your folks?' Nic had noticed them sitting not far from them.

Rose took a breath. 'Only if you keep things simple, don't say much, don't dare to mention the marriage, or that thing you did with Michael. Did you really take a selfie?'

'Not quite.'

'But you had your phone out, held his shoulder and everything.'

'I'll show you if you don't believe me.' Nic pulled his phone from his jacket pocket and opened it to the last picture. It was a photo of Dimond and the two girls.

Rose claimed. 'You reversed it.'

'Yep, and I showed Michael that I had taken the picture too. That's when he realised it was not in his best interest to keep pursuing you. There is something about Dimond though, something familiar. You are right she is very pretty, in a girl next door type of way. Oh, I've got it now, she's your doppelganger.'

Nic took the phone from Rose's gaze, scrolled to

the Vita Brevis dating site, and showed her the picture. 'See, no wonder she looks familiar.'

Rose looked at the portrait. 'That's me, and that's my Vita Brevis photo that Sandy had uploaded.'

'Yep, it is. You both have the same soft brown curls and the same soft eyes. You both look like you weigh around one-seventy-five, both late twenties, and almost the same shape. I mean yours is much neater, but it's almost the same as everything. He still wants to be married to you, Rose, but settled for Dimond instead.'

Nic then flicked to another shot of Rose. This one was a full-body shot of her standing next to the Mercedes 300SL. It was a classically beautiful pose he had taken earlier today.

'When did you take that?'

'In an unguarded moment. Besides your nose is so much prettier. I like a retroussé nose, and yours has it in spades.' He tapped Rose's nose with his forefinger and she glared at him. 'Please don't ever do that again.'

'I will, definitely, maybe, not ever do that again.'

'OK, Nic, you win. Let's go and meet them. I don't think you could do anything more embarrassing than the pantomime that we just had upstairs.'

'Do you want a bet?'

They were making their way over, and Nic detoured toward the couple from GOMA to acknowledge them. They beckoned him to sit, but he declined.

Nic and Rose arrived at the table of Rose's parents.

Her father stood to greet them and held out his hand, but her mother remained sitting.

'Zachariah Emmerson Palmer. Tell me, son, how long have you known our Rose?' They shook hands, and Zachariah sat down, but he didn't offer a seat to Nic or Rose.

'Call me Nic, pleased to meet you, sir. Rose has told me so much about you.' Nic quickly maneuvered out of the way to avoid Rose's incoming elbow jab, and then Rose's mother offered her hand, palm downwards, for Nic to kiss it. 'Jana Wilkinson. I am Rose's mother, and you didn't answer my husband's question.' Nic turned her hand over and shook it instead.

'Well, I don't like to talk about time Jana, after all, it is so fleeting. We don't live long enough to worry about the moments we take a breath, after all, it is the moments that take our breath away, isn't it?'

Nic noticed Jana had not responded to his idiom and was surprised as it was one of his best. He had read it on the back of a toilet door in London during his gap year. It has stayed with him ever since. It was a large door.

There was an uncomfortable silence, which her Father broke, as he took note Nic had stopped at the table of the GOMA couple. 'So, Nic, why were you talking with the Head of GOMA? I would not expect that any friend of Rose's would know anything about modern art.'

'Well, Zachariah. I work with a highly skilled team

of investors and we are always looking out for the next big venture. My equity partners are up from Sydney next week looking for another opportunity. Do you know of anybody that we could have a chat with?'

Zachariah was suddenly very interested, leaned forward, and looked over to Jana. 'Certainly, young man, my business interests are always looking for private equity partners.'

Rose knew that this was not going to end well, so she put her hand on Nic's arm. 'Let's not talk business in here please, Nic. We still have the will reading to get to. Perhaps you can all catch up later.'

On the way out Nic whispered to Rose. 'Why hasn't your mother taken the Palmer name?'

Rose stopped momentarily. 'Jana Palmer? Reverse the names around, Nic.'

Nic understood. 'That would mean your mother's name is Palmer-Jana....I should have said nice to '*m e a t*' you instead.' Rose softly punched him in the shoulder, and together they headed off towards Riparian Plaza to the next soirée.

Nic could see Rose was still seething about the modern art comment from her father, and Rose started up again. 'Aren't they just wonderful? I mean you have met my parents for less than five minutes, and they've already decided that you are too good for me.' Rose stopped mid-stride and watched as her parents drove past in a Rolls Royce.

Nic turned and stood in front of her, holding her

both shoulders. 'Yep Rose, sometimes life sucks, and you may have got served a giant bowl of lemons. So, take the sour fruit, stick it on the side of the salted glass and drink the tequila with big gulps. You are not your folks. You are you, and you are very worthy of everything that you can get out of this limited time we have here on this little revolving rock. The sun will come up tomorrow, and who knows what it will bring.'

'Damn you, Nic. Can't you stop being so positive? Is it the drugs? Tell me it's the drugs, and you're not like this every day.'

Nic grinned. 'Not every day. I try to avoid taking the happy drugs on any day that ends in the letter 'y' as they make me sad.'

'That's stupid.'

Nic shook his head. 'No more stupid than your Father's comment. He doesn't know me. He doesn't know us, or even if we are an us.' They started walking again and Rose began to whistle.

Nic smiled. 'You know Monty Python Rose?' as he had recognised the melody. "Always look on the bright side of life."

Rose grinned. 'Yes, that I do, but this is not the place for an argument.' Rose then launched into her version of a silly walk. 'John Cleese and the Minister for Silly Walks always cracks me up. The first time I did it around my father's office I was banished for weeks. I was twenty-four at the time.' Nic soon joined in with his version, and other pedestrians were avoiding them whilst they made their way further down the street.

As they walked past The Pig and Whistle Pub, Nic could hear a Beatles song being played live by the resident musician, and he stopped to listen. Rose kept walking so called her back. 'Have we got time for a quick drink before the will reading?'

'Yes, it's on from six, for a six-thirty start. So, maybe one, or two, or more, if you keep feeding me with all the mushy meaning of life crap.'

Nic nodded. 'Now that's a great Monty Python film that one.'

They sat on stools close to the stage and ordered a couple of Sam Adams. The muso continued with Beatles songs and finished with a simplified version of "Yesterday."

Nic went up to him and they started to chat. Rose could overhear them talking about The Beatles' repertoire and wanted to join in, then thought perhaps it was something she could work on if this thing with Nic went any further.

Meantime, Nic and the muso were getting quite animated, and it appeared they were going to do a duet. Nic turned to the crowd that had now quietened down a little and asked for their assistance. 'More Beatles or some Oasis?' compelling the crowd to get involved. It was getting noisier with all the shouting out.

Nic hushed them down and asked them to take a vote. 'Those who want more Beatles say "Yeah, Yeah,

Yeah," and those who want Oasis say "Maybe."' The Oasis crowd won out, the muso had a laugh and told them he was to play the song 'Wonderwall' if no one had objections.

Nic returned to the table, took a large gulp of his beer, took off his jacket, loosened his tie, gave Rose a wink, and turned back to the muso. 'But only if you let me play along with you.' Nic lifted the second guitar strap over his shoulder, and Rose recognised it as a 12-string acoustic. Nic plucked a pick from the microphone stand, attached a metal thingy to the neck, and started strumming out the song.

It was a good sound for an impromptu duo performance, and after one extended Wonderwall song later, including the endless playing of the chorus along with the singing crowd joining in, Nic put down the guitar, did some hand folding, shaking thing with the muso, slipped a fifty dollar note into the glass bowl at the foot of the stage, and chugged the last of his beer.

They finally made their way out to the footpath and Rose looked at Nic. 'I didn't know you played. It wasn't in your profile. How did you know he would let you play?'

'Well, I have to confess I know him. We used to jam together years ago. It may have been a little rusty in parts, but think we still have a good sound.'

'It was a good version of the song, but I didn't know The Beatles did that one.'

CHAPTER 4

The Will Reading was up on the 30th floor, and Nic was busying himself putting back on his jacket and tie as they ascended the lift. Rose patted his lapels down as the doors opened, and they stepped into the foyer of the empty lawyer's office.

They went over to the floor-to-ceiling windows and looked out at the view. It was a panoramic vision of the Brisbane River, starting from the Storey Bridge on the left, along the Kangaroo Point cliffs and down to the Captain Cook Bridge. Several river ferries were operating below, and the Brisbane River Queen Paddle Wheelers transporting tonight's sightseers were just leaving their quay.

'It's a beautiful city isn't it, Rose?'

They continued to watch the business of late afternoon Brisbane from above. 'I do miss it when I am away, and that's why I love coming home.'

'So, Brisbane is your home then?'

'Sort of, and yes, I do have an apartment at Southbank. I was born and raised in a small country town in Victoria. I also have an apartment in Adelaide and access to a property in Melbourne. You could say that my home is where my heart is, well, at least where my suitcases are anyway.'

'That is so clichéd, Nic.'

Their conversation was interrupted by a young man approaching them from within the confines of the office suites. 'Rosemary Palmer, we are waiting for you, Rosemary Palmer are you here?'

'You didn't tell me your name was Rosemary?'

Nic held his finger in the air and gained the man's attention. 'And that must have been difficult for him to work out, given that we are the only two people standing out here.'

'Behave, Nic. He is just doing his job.'

The young man introduced himself as Cody and indicated the need to follow him to the boardroom. As they passed through the corridors, Nic noticed the imposing portraits of the Managing Partners displayed along the walls. 'Cody, I guess you hope to have your picture up here one day too?'

'Not me sir, no. Those people look too old.'

They struggled to keep up with him, so Nic slowed down to see if Cody would notice - he didn't, and they were now standing still. 'So Rose. Do I call you Rose, Rosie, Rosemary? Tomorrow? After all, they say a rose by any other name.'

Rose jabbed at his ribs. 'Rose is fine. Please stop with the attempted comedy routine. It's about to get serious.'

Cody eventually noticed they weren't following so hurried them up, and then led them through the myriad of offices. They finally reached a pair of solid oak doors. "The Boardroom" was emblazoned in gold lettering across the two doors. Cody rapped lightly on them, announced that he had located the latecomers and opened the right-hand side door, which left the other side closed. It read "THE BO."

Rose felt Nic was about to say something. 'Not now, and please keep your little comments to yourself. This may get ugly. Just behave and keep quiet.'

Nic grinned. 'That's not fair, Rose. I have always thought a '+1' is meant to add something.'

Rose and Nic found two seats next to each other at the table. There were ten people on each side including Zachariah, Jana, Sandy, the two Stephens and others he did not know or recognise from the funeral. Michael and Dimond were there too along with the couple from GOMA, and there was also a distinguished-looking gentleman sitting at the head. Nic recognised him from a portrait they had passed in the corridor and whispered to Rose. 'I have seen his picture somewhere recently, but I can't work out where. Jail? A wanted ad at the Post Office? ATO tax evasion club?'

'Sshh Nic. I won't ask you again, otherwise you are out.'

The man stood up and introduced himself. 'Welcome, I am Grantley De Souza. Welcome to Pipers. We are all here this evening for the reading of the Last Will and Testament of Charles Albert Brown. I am normally required to read the following *plene peficere*, but in the interest of time have, provided a copy of the Statements of Survivorship. You may know Albert never married and both of his parents have passed. He has no living relatives, did not have any children and this firm was appointed as the Trustee of the Estate. The will is fairly simple, and only contains five items of mention.'

Nic leaned into Rose again. 'His real name was Charlie Brown. No wonder he used Albert and all the other's names, and there are eighteen people in here looking for their piece of the pie. I do hope there is a lot to go around, especially for Linus and Snoopy, as they were his best friends after all. I have excluded myself of course.'

Rose whispered. 'Nic, please keep quiet.'

The lawyer continued through the usual declarations from the will reading, then finally said he had reached the statement of bequests. Nic watched as a number of them moved forward in their chairs, and noticed that Rose had not moved. Her arms were still crossed over her chest. Sandy had not moved either.

<u>Item 1/</u>

I Bequeath the SUM of $250,000 to my nephew Simeon Walden Wadlow, of 19 The Boulevard NHILL in the State of Victoria.

Everyone took a breath.

The lawyer stopped after that reading and declared that they had not been able to locate any such person of that name. He confirmed that Albert did not have any siblings or known relatives, and therefore believed this bequest to be invalid.

<u>Item 2/</u>

I Bequeath the BRETT WHITELEY PAINTING known as BIG BLUE, LAVENDER BAY to the Gallery of Modern Art (GOMA) Brisbane. It is currently situated at the property of Zachariah and Jana Palmer, of 17 Killara Avenue HAMILTON in the State of Queensland.

The lawyer stopped after that reading, declared the painting is considered suspect due to the ongoing investigation as to its authenticity, and again clarified that this bequest was invalid.

Nic had been wondering why the couple from GOMA were present, and Rose whispered; 'It's a fake, Nic.'

<u>Item 3/</u>

I Bequeath the PROPERTY situated at 1113A Brett's Wharf HAMILTON to my niece SANDRA FRASER, of 68 Hill End Terrace WEST END in the State of Queensland.

The lawyer stopped after that reading and declared that although it was a valid bequest, the property no longer existed as it had been resumed by the State of Queensland to build the Kingsford Smith Drive deviation and new ferry stop. He again confirmed this bequest to be invalid.

Nic watched Sandy's reaction assuming she was the Sandra named in the bequest.

Rose whispered, 'Yes, she is Nic. Nice gesture, but a bit late don't you think?'

<u>Item 4/</u>

I Bequeath the RACEHORSE known as ELEGANT BEAUTY currently situated at the ROYAL EQUEST-IAN CENTRE BOWEN HILLS to my niece ROSEMARY PALMER of 68 Hill End Terrace WEST END in the State of Queensland.

Nic looked over to Rose. Neither her expression nor posture had changed, so he whispered; 'Aw, he left you a little horsey.'

'Not exactly Nic. It died over three months ago.'

<u>Item 5/</u>

I Bequeath the remainder of my Estate to Zachariah and Jana Palmer of 17 Killara Avenue HAMILTON in the State of Queensland.

This time Rose smiled at that bequest, and Nic noticed. 'Why are you smiling?

'Well, that means they have become the rightful owner of all the stuff that Albert has stored under our house. Mother was always nagging him to have it removed, but he'd often said it all meant too much to him. Now they have to pay for it to be taken away.'

The lawyer then brought the party to the atten-tion of the review of the Bank Accounts held at the

Common Bank Branch, Racecourse Road, Hamilton. 'I have managed to locate one Bank Account held by the deceased. It contained the sum in the entirety of $19.10.'

Rose laughed out loud this time, and her parents noticed. Nic whispered. 'Rose, behave, otherwise I will have you thrown out, and don't think I'm serious.'

Michael suddenly stood up. 'This must be a mistake. I would not have wasted my time coming to the reading.' Dimond was trying to settle him down, but he continued to rant. 'Where is the rest of the money? The old fool promised I was in the will. How can it all be gone? You two, Rosemary and Sandra, what did you do with my share?'

Rose stood up and walked over to Sandy who was sitting there quietly, holding her hands to the side of her face. Sandy looked up at Michael. 'It's all gone Michael; he lost it when the shop closed. It was mortgaged to the hilt, and what the government paid him barely covered the payout to the Bank. The rest went on his care. You know he spent the last few months in respite at RBH, how do think that was all paid for?'

Michael remained standing but wanted more. He kept gesturing around to each person at the table, but when he locked eyes on Nic, he promptly sat down muttering something about not knowing why Rose had brought Nic along. Rose looked at Nic. 'See, and that's why I needed a +1 this afternoon,' and she came back around to sit down next to him.

The reading then quickly dissolved, leaving Rose, Sandy and Nic sitting alone.

Sandy began to explain to Nic why the shop had to close; "The She Shed" was everything to him Nic, it made him feel important, made him feel that he could look people in the eye and say he was an investor. He had faith in our little business, and we appreciated the opportunity, but it closed. The government took it away, and then it took him away.'

Sandy began to cry, and Rose began crying too.

Two crying women. Nic didn't quite know where to look or what to do, so he decided it was the best time to leave. He wished them both well, walked out, caught the ferry from the Eagle Street stop, and went home to his apartment at Southbank. As he disembarked, he wondered if he would ever see Rose and Sandy again. He had found them both so beguiling.

CHAPTER 5

Sandy and Rose left the lawyer's office and exited the building. 'Are you hungry Rose? George's Paragon Restaurant will still be open. Do you want to eat there?'

'Friday night. It'll be busy, so how about we have a pint at the Bavarian Beer Café while we wait for a table?'

'Yes. That sounds like a plan.'

They went up the escalators to the first level, approached the maître de at Georges, and were told there was about an hour to wait. A flute of champagne was offered, and they were handed a "Your Table is Ready" buzzer. They found a couple of stools at an outside table, and the view was across the river to the Storey Bridge.

'Look, Sandy, it's Michael, Dimond and the girls.' Rose nodded down to him and the family that were walking along the promenade down below. Michael was remonstrating about something and his group were trying their best to keep up with him. The family finally stopped directly underneath where Rose and Sandy were sitting.

'It's not fair. He promised me Di, he looked me square in the face and told me I'd get something. He was talking about eighty thousand dollars, so I went and bought the new BMW Z3 Convertible. I was going to surprise you with it for your birthday.'

'I saw you looking at that car Michael. It's only a two-door. Where do Skye and Lucy sit? It doesn't have any rear seats.'

Michael shook his head. 'That's not the point, Di. It was what I wanted. Stuff the girls, they won't be with us much longer anyway.'

'Dad, I'm only nine. Where am I going to go?' Skye said fiercely, and then Lucy started crying.

Dimond sighed. 'Daddy is just ranting guys. You're not going anywhere. He'll take that silly little car back.' Upon hearing that, Michael stormed off leaving his family standing there.

Sandy looked at Rose. 'You were once married to him, weren't you, Rose?'

'Yes, unfortunately.'

'So ...and you know ... what Nic said before....was it?'

Rose took a sip of her champagne and considered her reply. 'No, of course not,' then she burst out laughing. 'I wouldn't let him get anywhere near me. He is disgusting, it was disgusting, all of it, and I'm never going to get married again. Tried it once, didn't like it.'

Sandy nodded. 'What about Nic then? Where does he fit into all of this?'

'+1 that's all. He was good today, and we got lucky there.'

Sandy nodded. 'Are you going to see him again?'

Rose shrugged. 'I don't know. Hey, I just thought of something. I can't ever marry him either.'

'Oh, why not?'

Rose grinned. 'Nic Thorn marries Rose Palmer....that will make me Rose Thorn,' and they both burst out laughing. Rose's phone then chimed, she glanced at it, but the restaurant buzzer started going off.

'Our table is ready Sandy.'

They moved back inside, were shown to a table near a window and whilst perusing the menu, Sandy looked at her now empty glass, then called a waiter over to their table. 'May we please have another two flutes of the champagne? What was it?'

'Moet, I believe madam.'

Sandy nodded. 'That's fine then. Thank you.'

Rose leaned forward. 'It's twenty dollars a glass. I don't think the funds they said Uncle Albert had left will cover that.'

'Don't worry about it, Rose. I'll cover it. There is something that you should know about Uncle Albert's estate. There was only one Bank Account, but I had Power of Attorney. It was all legit, as everything was co-signed by the lawyer, Grant. I mean all the money is gone as there was the cost of keeping him in the RBH, but I was always paying for stuff, and we had to lodge a deposit for his initial admission too. That all went back to the lawyers, not directly to his estate when he died. There is a little bit more to draw from before it runs out. Maybe just enough to cover tonight's meal, and a night at the Palazzo Versace down the coast too if you would like.'

'So what, a couple of thousand?'

'Closer to three, but I'm sure what's leftover will be lost in legal fees anyway.'

They ordered dinner. Sandy had the Avocado Seafood followed by the Seafood Crepe, and Rose selected the Greek Salad & Five in One.

'Don't you love it here Rose, the waiters are around, but don't hover. This place is always busy, and the food is never disappointing.'

'So, tell me about Nic then. How long have you known him?'

'What is the time now?' Sandy looked at her phone. 'About nine-thirty.'

Rose continued: 'OK. I saw him for about half an hour this morning, then he picked me up at three. We went to the funeral, the wake and then the reading. He left at about seven-thirty. So that makes it five hours in total."

'What? Not before today?'

'No, I needed a +1 and he was it, and that was it. Maybe there could be more, but I don't know yet.'

'What? Don't like your men dark, handsome and mysterious?'

Rose grinned. 'No. I prefer them short, fat and shallow…just what my parents ordered when they hooked me up with Michael.'

'I think you need to get over it, Rose. This Nic guy just might be your knight in shining armour.'

'Yes, he could be. He even rides in a white pony.'

'What?'

'He drives a white Ford Mustang, and they do call them a pony.' Rose then shrugged again. 'But, I don't know how to get in touch with him other than through the dating app. I guess we should call it a night and go home. I don't want to go to Hamilton tonight though. Not ever again really. I'll come back with you to West End instead.'

Sandy smiled. 'Sure.'

Rose opened her phone, and called for an Uber, then noticed that there was a missed call and a message. She listened to the call and read the SMS which was from Nic, then she smiled and showed it to Sandy. 'I didn't even give him my number.'

In the morning, Sandy and Rose walked along the river towards the city, under the Kurilpa Bridge and turned into Grey Street in front of the Queensland Performing Arts Centre where the B R I S B A N E signage was displayed on the lawn.

'Where would you like to have breakfast, Sandy?'

'Let's try the Cafés near Stokehouse. Haven't been there for ages.'

They made their way through the Southbank paths, arrived at the River café, and unexpectedly recognized one of the patrons sitting at a front table casually sipping on a cup of tea.

It was Nic.

CHAPTER 6

'Morning guys. This is my morning hangout place. I wasn't expecting to see you here too.' Nic stood up and welcomed them both with a European greeting. 'And Rose, you didn't respond to my call or my text. I assumed it was all over between us, but here you are. I need a big favour.'

Rose looked at Sandy, then cautiously back to Nic. 'OK....tell us about it.'

'Well, I have a meeting with the Head of GOMA in about an hour and I need to set something up within the gallery that may involve a diversion. They believe something is suspicious with one of the art pieces, and it needs to be verified. It would normally be attended to by their security, but even they are under scrutiny at the moment, and want me to have a look instead."

'What do you need us to do?'

'Nothing at the moment. I just need to know if you are both available to help me out if needed. I'll pay you and meet any expenses, though there shouldn't be any. Oh, and you might need a change of clothes as there is a chance you might get wet. I'll explain a bit more later though.'

Nic then stretched his legs out and placed his hands behind his head. 'The city view is spectacular from this side of the river too, isn't it?'

They discussed the new Queens Wharf precinct currently under construction and agreed they didn't know where the people would come from to fill it all. Sandy wanted to know if he had stayed at the new Weston Hotel, but Rose piped up instead.

'I booked myself in there once and managed to pick up a two-night stay including a pamper package for less than five hundred dollars. King bed and everything."

'Everything?' Nic enquired with a raise of his eyebrow.

'Behave, Nic. God, I am sick of saying that to you.'

'But you're not sick of seeing me yet are you, Rose?'

Sandy quickly interjected. 'You know you two have only known each other for five hours, and already you are behaving like an old married couple.'

Rose turned to face Sandy, then casually turned back to Nic. 'And if you ever ask me to marry you. Don't, I don't ever want to be a Rose Thorn.'

Nic laughed and stood up. 'You guys haven't had breakfast yet have you?'

Rose sighed. 'No.'

'Tell you what, I have to go to this meeting now, so I'll settle the bill. Please stay here, as the Avo on

Toast is to die for. I have your mobile numbers, so I'll be in touch.'

Sandy watched as he walked along the promenade heading toward GOMA. 'He is a mighty fine something, Rose. I don't know quite what it is, but there is something mighty fine about him.'

'Hey, stop staring in case he looks back here. We don't want that, and by the way, when did you give him your mobile number?'

'I didn't.'

They went to the bar to pay and found that Nic had already done so. 'I don't like that, Sandy. It's sneaky. How did he know we were going to stay here, and how much it would cost? Damn you again, Nic.' They moved back out of the café and stood on the promenade. 'What are we going to do now, Sandy?'

They watched the CityCats traversing the river. 'Let's take a ferry around to Eagle Street, and catch the cross-river ferry to the Jazz Club under the Storey Bridge. One of my friends is playing there tonight, and has a couple of free tickets for us.'

They arrived at the Jazz Club. Sandy went up to the cashier and mentioned the name of her friend. The cashier searched around eventually finding a single ticket with a yellow sticky note attached. *"For Sandy."* The cashier handed it over. 'Sorry Sandy, it's only one ticket. Your friend will have to pay the full tote. Forty for the show or sixty for the show, and two drinks.' Rose shook her head. 'Sandy, if it's OK, I might just stay home and clean up the house as a thank you for letting me stay with you at such short notice.'

They started to move away when Rose's phone rang and then Sandy's phone rang. They looked at each other. It was Nic calling both numbers, so they found a table nearby, sat down and placed the phones face up. 'Yes, Nic.'

'Ah, my Angels. Thank you for taking my call?'

Sandy leaned into Rose. 'Are we supposed to call him Charlie now?'

Nic overheard and laughed. 'No, I am still Nic, but where are you?'

Sandy leaned forward again. 'Jazz Club, Kangaroo Point.'

'Right, I know it well. There is a band playing to-night that I would like to see. One of my friends is in it. I think the group is called 'The Salted Plums', or something like that.'

Sandy leaned forward again. 'Nic, they are called 'The Sweetened Plums', and one of my friends is in the band, too.'

'Oh, what is his name?'

'The him is a her, Nic. The lead singer is Carly McCullough. Who's your friend?'

'The drummer, Sticks Out. We call him that because of his big ears.'

Rose leaned forward this time. 'That's not nice Nic, and I bet they don't play Oasis as good as you either.'

'Hey Rose, it's Jazz. They don't play other people's

songs. It's all made up on the spot. Anyway, are you guys free around eleven tomorrow? I need to run through this thing at GOMA to see if it will work.'

They looked at each other and nodded. 'Yes, that will work for us, so see you then.' They closed the calls, looked at each other, and wondered what to do next. Sandy smiled. 'Not having a day job works for me, Rose.'

Rose was a little pensive with her response. 'Why do think Nic mentioned there was a chance we could get wet? How about we check out GOMA right now if that's OK? I want to see what we are getting ourselves into with Nic tomorrow.'

They hopped back on the City Hopper, alighted at Southbank, made their way down to GOMA and entered the foyer where an exhibition called 'WATER' was showing.

Rose approached one of the attendants and asked to explain it to her. 'Thank you for asking. All the artists are using water as their muse. There is a room made up of a vast rocky riverbed, another exhibition of plastic pipes dispensing frothy soap, and one entire room with a cascading waterfall operating on a con-stant recycling basis. Plus a few other watery things.'

Sandy took one of the brochures and read aloud the definition of the exhibition to Rose. 'It all seems a little arty farty to me, so I wonder how Nic wants us involved?' They left GOMA and went back home to West End.

Around 8 pm Sandy came out of her bedroom. 'Come on Rose, the Jazz music will be fun, and if you discount Nic, what fun have you had lately? Besides I might be able to sweet talk the cashier into letting you in for free too, seeing we know Nic's friend.'

'Sorry Sandy. I'm still not up to it, but I'll drive you there if you like.'

They jumped into their little Nissan S Cargo Van. It was still covered with the decals of "The She Shed", and they both had tapped at the doors before climbing in as it still meant so much to them. The car was about fifteen years old but was very maneuverable around the city for deliveries. They still couldn't bear to part with it.

It took longer than they thought, so it was just before 8.45 pm when Rose dropped her off, but the show had not started, and there was still a lineup to get in. Rose wound down the window. 'Would you like me to pick you up later?'

'No, I'll Uber it as I don't know what time it will finish up.'

'Remember, we have this thing with Nic at eleven, so don't be out too late. We don't know what we have to do. Be prepared for anything.'

Sandy dodged her way past the waiting throng and managed to get inside. She saw a "band table" was set up just left of the stage, made her way over there and sat down on one of the stools. A scruffy young man came up and started drumming a paradiddle against the side of her table.

'You must be Sticks Out.'

'That's me. What gave it away - my drumsticks or my ears?'

'I didn't know about your ears until Nic Thorn told me. I am here for Carly.'

'Carly hey, that's interesting, and you know Nic too, the man; the legend; the - well whatever he is up to now. How do you know him?'

'I met him today, but don't know anything about him. Can you enlighten me?'

'I could, but I have undertaken a vow of silence with the secrets of Nic Thorn;' and before she could respond, other members of the band came up. Carly gave Sandy a greeting kiss, then the band entered the stage area to start playing.

Meantime, back at Hill End Rose couldn't sleep. She didn't know if it was that Sandy wasn't home, or it was thinking about Nic. Rose rolled over, punched the pillow a couple of times, and turned the glowing red light of the old digital clock face down.

CHAPTER 7

Rose woke. It was morning and she hadn't heard Sandy come home, but she had managed some sleep. She turned up the clock and saw it was already 10 a.m., so quickly climbed in and out of the shower and threw on some clothes. Then realised that Nic had mentioned the possibility of getting wet, so discarded them and put on something else. *Where is Sandy?*

It was now getting later. Sandy still wasn't around and she wasn't answering her phone either. She never turned it off, and always kept it charged using the charger on the kitchen cupboard. Rose gave up, dashed out through the door and realised she didn't have the car keys, so went back into the kitchen. As she collected them, noticed Sandy's phone charger, and then realised she might be doing the thing with Nic on her own.

Parking in the underground South Bank carpark between two Land Cruisers, Rose smiled at the irony that her little car cost the same to park here as those two behemoths. Nic had mentioned covering her expenses which may include the car parking, so made a mental note to get a receipt.

Fortunately, it was only about a five-minute walk from the car park to GOMA, so she quickened her walk and made it just before eleven. Rose brushed herself down, took a deep breath, and walked between the opening glass sliding doors. Nic was waiting in the foyer.

The same attendant that was there yesterday saw Rose, and said, 'Welcome back.' Nic overheard and walked up. 'I thought you said you haven't been here before.'

'I haven't, well not before yesterday anyway. Sandy and I came in to have a look around.'

'Mm, that is a little disappointing, I needed you to keep a low profile. Tell me how far you went in, and whether anybody else saw you.' Nic took her by the arm, led her towards the alcove by the toilets and sat her down. 'Tell me what you did, and start at the beginning. What time it was, who you saw, who saw you, and who you talked to.'

'I can't remember, Nic. I'm sorry. I didn't know what you wanted us to do. I was trying to make sure we would be safe. I mean, I have only known you for five hours.'

Nic nodded. 'OK, I give you that, but you have to admit Rose, it was a little.....' Rose sighed. 'Stupid?'

'No, I was just going to say naïve. I don't think I

would ever call someone that looks like you, stupid. It doesn't make sense.'

'Thanks, I guess.'

Nic used a softer tone now. 'So, tell me what you did, and how far you went in.'

'We didn't go in. We stopped here in the foyer. It was about elevenish as we hadn't yet eaten, and the only person I spoke to was that attendant over there. Um, Sandy took a brochure, and that's about it. Oh, by the way, do you know where Sandy is?'

Nic nodded. 'She is with Ian. He sent me a text -told me she wouldn't make it.'

'Ian who?'

'Oh sorry, I mean Sticks Out, the drummer, he's the guy with The Sweetened Plums. They got talking after the show and all went back to Carly's place at Milton. Sandy wanted to leave, but she had missed the last ferry, and it is a long walk around to Hill End that time of night, so she decided to stay the night.'

'So, Carly and Sticks Out live together?'

'The whole band does. Every time they change a band member over, they make the old one move out and move the new one in. They insist on them being single too, as they reckon family and children can get in the way. It's a little harsh, but whatever floats your boat, or in the case binds the band.'

Rose sighed. 'So we're good?'

'Yep,' Nic touched her nose with his forefinger.

'Please don't do that.'

'I can't avoid it. I mean your nose.... well it's perfect.'
Nic was about to explain about the gig but thought better of it as they were still in GOMA, so he led Rose back outside, and down the side of the building to the restaurant below.

'This is nice, Nic, but a bit expensive just for lunch.'

'Yep, but they do a great Chai Latte and a mean turkey with camembert on rye.'

They ordered and went back outside to find a table, hopefully not covered in the pesky ibis. Nic looked for a clean table. 'Damn those bin-chickens. There's one over there, closest to the sculpture of the elephant standing on its head.'

They sat, and Rose took a sip of her tea. 'So, what is this GOMA thing all about Nic? And why am I dressed like this just in case I get wet?'

Nic shook his head. 'No, not today. It's not happening today. We just have to set it up today. Do a recon to see if it will work, and what contingencies we have if it doesn't. Let's finish lunch, and go for a walk. I think the further we are away from GOMA, the better chance we have of not being overheard.'

They disposed of their rubbish and walked along the promenade towards the Kurilpa Bridge. Nic started up again. 'It's something to do with a suspect tapestry and the 'Heads Of' need me to take a scraping while in situ. I need a distraction to be able to get close enough to do it, and I have to step inside the blue cord that surrounds the front of the display without being seen.'

'Why can't you just take it off the wall and test it under clinical conditions?'

'The artist won't allow it.'

'OK, I'm convinced, but how will I be getting wet?'

'Well, inside the exhibition, there is a room that is just a waterfall and a pond, and you are going to fall into the water. It is being set up for Thursday as this is the day that the teenage boys for Brisbane Boys Grammar Year Eleven will be visiting. You will be emerging from the water dripping wet, and you'll only have a T-shirt and cut-off jeans on. You'll become the main attraction for a while, then I'll do my part on the tapestry in the room next door. Oh, and make sure you wear heels, nothing too high, as you still have to be able to walk around, and your mascara, it can't be waterproof.'

'Oh, OK, but how will you keep me safe amongst a pack of marauding teenage boys? Is there a chance that I well maybe, um, could it get out of control?'

Nic nodded. 'That is why we are here today, to go through the plan and the contingencies. So let's go back in and have a look. Thanks for trusting me, by the way.'

They went back in and another one of the attendants met them in the foyer. 'This is Everard and he is your 'go-to' guy in the waterfall room. Don't worry about him being part of the problem, as he's one of my men on the inside. He started about three months ago, and we have been working on getting him rostered into the waterfall room for the last month.'

Nic looked at him. 'So we are good for Thursday?'

The man nodded very subtly, and then they both looked over to the attendant that Rose had met. Nic whispered to Everard. 'Can you take care of that?'

Rose overheard. 'You are not going to kill her just because she met me, are you? That's horrible, surely you don't do that stuff too?'

'Not likely Rose, I'll never do that. Taking care of people is finding out people's weaknesses and leveraging them. In her case, she likes African animals and suddenly, she has an opportunity to spend three days at Australia Zoo in Beerwah, leaving on Tuesday. She won a competition, didn't she Everard?'

Again the man nodded very subtly and then he led them into the exhibition.

As it was currently closed for a minor refurbishment, they were free to move directly to the waterfall room. Rose looked at it, realised the pool was not that deep, and wondered how she was going to get wet. 'Do I have to roll around in the water to get wet ?'

'No Rose, the waterfall is currently turned off.'

Nic motioned for Everard to turn it on, and water then began gurgling at the end of the pond, siphoning through and cascading down the wall. Everard approached Rose as she leaned down to gauge the temperature of the water. Everard gently raised her hands from the pond but said nothing, rather he simply waved his hand at the water and shook his head sideways. Nic saw what was going on. 'Rose don't go anywhere near the pumps. You have to stay near the waterfall end.'

'OK, got it. So where will you be?'

'Next door. My work is in the next room. I'll need no more than five minutes, but there will be a lot going on in here with a room full of boys. Play it safe, and if you are in any doubt, you will have a safe word to walk away. Let's make it "bond". My word is my bond, that will work, Rose.'

Everard finally spoke in a low gravelly tone, and Rose looked shocked. 'I'll be carrying you out of the water ma'am. You'll be safe with me, so don't panic when you see me climbing into the pond to rescue you.'

'But won't you get wet too?'

'Nope, as long as you don't splash me, and I'll be covering you with my coat as soon as I can, for your...um, dignity.'

'OK, so I have until Thursday to change my mind, Nic?'

'Nope, right now.'

'So, what's with the 'bond', safe word stuff then?'

'That is only for Thursday. I'll be going ahead with my task regardless of what happens to you. Are you in, Rose?' Rose looked at Nic, looked at Everard, looked at the waterfall, which had now been turned off, and nodded. 'OK, I'm in.'

They went around the rear of the waterfall, and Nic showed Rose to the Emergency Exit doors. It was dark at the back of the display as it was shrouded in a black curtain. 'This is where Everard will carry you to. It leads outside.'

Rose went to open the doors to have a look, but Everard quickly grasped her hands. 'It's alarmed ma'am, so you can't go through now.'

Nic took over. 'OK Rose, the timing has to be right for the diversion because your little fall into the waterfall is only the first chain in the link. The alarm will be sounding when you are carried through the corridor and that should bring some of the other attendants out of the room that I'll be in. The school boys will need to be contained and there is a chance it could all go awry. You start your show at exactly eleven-o-five, as that is when you need to fall into the water. I don't care how you do it, just make sure you get wet. You might have to count down and I'll get you a watch with a couple of countdown timers and an alarm on it. It has to be three minutes. At eleven-o-eight, Everard will be in there with you, and carrying you out of there. At eleven-ten, he'll open the Emergency Doors and the alarm will sound. It is loud so be prepared for it. Everard will only be dumping you back outside. You will need to make your way home and don't forget to give his jacket back. Pack lightly as everything will be getting wet. If your phone is destroyed, I'll be replacing it too.'

'The cameras Nic. What about the cameras in here?'

'At the moment they are off. That's why we needed to be here now. I arranged some scheduled maintenance, and backup of the security system this morning.'

'But what about yesterday's camera vision of me and Sandy?'

'Could be an issue, but unlikely as you were not here long, and only in the foyer.'

'What about Thursday though? How are you going to avoid them then?'

'Boy, you ask a lot of questions. Thursday will be different. All the cameras will be on, and the one directly on my tapestry will be marginally shifted to re-direct the view. So, other than that, are we good to go?'

'I have some more questions, Nic.' Everard and Nic rolled their eyes, and Nic continued: 'Not in here, Rose. We have to go. Everard has to get back to work. Let's go and have a coffee and you can ask me then. Where would you like to go?'

'San Churro in Grey Street.'

'When in doubt go to chocolate?'

'Yes, always.'

Nic took a breath. 'You know I was struggling a little to come up with the best plan, Rose, but you and

Dimond inspired me. I'm going to use the "Doppelganger principle"'.

'What?'

'Well, my team is all going to be dressed the same,
same blue jeans; same Bronco's cap; same coloured
t-shirt and reefer jackets.'

'Won't you all be easy to spot all dressed like that?'

'Not quite, as there is a little more to it than that,
but it'll work. So, after today's lunch, I won't be back
in touch with you until Saturday. Just keep a low
profile. Don't go back to GOMA - avoid South Bank
altogether if you can.'

They sat down to lunch. Rose ordered a hug-mug,
followed by the chocolate pizza. Nic stuck with water.
'Nic, what about Sandy? Won't you have to get her up
to speed on this too?'

'Err. No. You will be on your own. Didn't she tell
you that The Sweetened Plums have got a gig for a
couple of days down at the Star Casino Gold Coast?
They have already left.'

Rose shook her head. 'No, I haven't seen or heard
from her since yesterday, and her phone charger is at
home on the kitchen sink.'

Nic nodded. 'I got a text from Sticks Out. It sounds
like they are all getting on. Do you want to give him a
call instead?'

Rose smiled. 'No, that's OK. Sandy wanted to get
into the Band Management stuff one day.'

'Tough gig. Been there done that.'

Rose sighed. 'Is it any tougher than me emerging dripping wet in front of a pack of marauding teenage boys?'

Nic grinned. 'Touché, Rose.'

Rose only ate half of the pizza and pushed it forward on the table, 'I'm finished,' and with that, they stood up to leave. Nic gave her a quick peck on the cheek and jogged away. As he left, she realised something. 'Hey Nic, I still don't have your number,' but he was already out of earshot.

CHAPTER 8

On Thursday morning Rose was staring at herself in the bathroom mirror. *"You can do this Rose. It's only getting a bit wet, standing in front of teenage boys, having some man carrying you, and then getting dumped outside like a drowned rat. I mean you just had a shower. How hard can it be?"*

Rose had found some non-waterproof mascara and was busy applying it when she stopped and looked at herself again. A single tear started falling from her eye, so automatically reacted by wiping it away with the back of her hand. When she looked again, she noticed it had entirely smeared her eyelid, so she straightened her back and stood to her full height. *"Pull yourself together, you can do this."*

A small parcel had arrived earlier in the week which she had been reluctant to open. It was the watch, but she didn't know anything about it or how to work it. Rose had given up that jewellery item years ago. *"I like my little phone. I mean it's an Apple SE. I don't want a new one. I just have to make sure it doesn't get wet."*

Rose caved in and opened the box with the watch.

There was a yellow note folded underneath. "Don't push this button until Thursday. The watch will chime at 11.00, then again at 11.05, and again at 11.08." There was another note in there - this one was white. "P.S. I knew you would not open this box until Thursday." Rose shrugged. *'Damn, you Nic.'*

She pulled on the pair of cut-off denim shorts that had been requested, then next, the white T-shirt. Staring at it on the bed she couldn't remember if Nic had said she needed to be bra-less, so put those on too. Then thought about it, and took them off, then thought about it again, and put them back on. She found the shoes that she could bear to lose, strapped them on, and found a matching clutch.

Rose was ready but felt something was missing from the outfit. She wanted to look a little bookish; not librarian bookish; but Post-Grad bookish. Glasses, reading glasses - the rounder the better. She didn't wear them, but perhaps Sandy had a pair. Rose paused at Sandy's bedroom door, but she didn't have a choice, it was an emergency after all.

Rose opened the door and stepped into the room. Everything was tidy. The bed was made and there was nothing else on the top of the dresser apart from a picture of Rose and Sandy taken by Uncle Albert standing together in front of "The She Shed" on the day it opened. Rose turned the portrait face down to alleviate some of the guilt of being in Sandy's room. 'Sorry Sandy but this is an emergency. Blame Nic, not me.'

Finding a glass jar containing some reading glasses, Rose took the jar from the room, shut the door, sat down at the kitchen table and took a deep breath.

The five pairs in the jar were now scattered across the kitchen table. Eliminating the Dame Edna pair was easy. That left four. Two were a little grubby, and they looked like men and Rose wondered why Sandy had kept them. *"How could a man that wears glasses get up in the morning from whatever happened the night before, and leave without them? I don't get men"*, Rose said aloud to acknowledge the spectacle of lost loves.

That left two: A Buddy Holly pair and a pair of Ray-Bans. She tried the Ray-Bans on first and moved over to the toaster to look at its reflective surface. Rose decided that they would suit, left them on, grabbed the clutch, and her phone, saw the time was about 9.30, and headed off.

On the way out she saw the neighbour and stopped to have a chat. 'Hi Dave, how have you been?' Dave nodded. 'Good. Everything's good, thanks, Rose. Sorry to hear about 'The She Shed' and Uncle Albert, though.' They made some more small talk, and then Dave asked her about her glasses. 'I didn't know that you wore reading glasses.'

Rose nodded. 'Nope. Trying them out today.' Dave smiled. 'OK, but you do know that they don't have any lenses in them, don't you?'

Rose took them off, looked at them, nodded at Dave, and scurried back inside to grab the Buddy Holly ones. Fortunately, they were just glass, without any prescription.

It was now 10.20, and Rose was standing outside GOMA. The panic was starting to set in, and she hadn't seen Nic anywhere. This was a good thing. She hadn't seen people all dressed the same either, which was probably a good thing too.

The exhibit queue extended a lot further than she had hoped, it snaked back around on itself and didn't seem to be moving. Rose looked at the watch, and it now showed 10.45, but fortunately, the line thinned out as several patrons were ushered out. 'What's going on?' Rose enquired of the lady in front of her.

'Oh, that group just realised they have pre-paid their tickets. It's a separate lane if you bought your tickets online.'

Damn it Nic, why didn't you tell me I could do that?

Finally arriving at the front of the queue, she handed over the entry fee in cash, asked for a receipt and stepped through with ten minutes to spare. Rose looked for the Bronco Caps or tried to catch someone dressed alike, then was ushered out of the way though as a group of children went past her. Rose smiled at them as she realised they were all wearing the Bronco's Caps - then overheard one of them saying about not missing out, and that they could get one from the big box on the way out as they were being given away for free in the foyer.

With five minutes to go, she made her way into the waterfall room, deliberately ignoring Everard near the side exit, and even evaded some of the BBC boys who were huddled around the pond. The watch chimed 11, and she realised it had never occurred to her that it would happen.

Just how am I going to do this?

One of the groups of boys near her started waving their hands around at something they were watching on an iPad. Rose looked over to Everard for guidance but he ignored her. Apparently, it was a picture of a schoolgirl in a bikini, so then she turned away and now had her back to them. The watch was about to chime at 11.05, so she leaned backwards into the group of boys, they pushed back and this was the opportunity she needed, just enough momentum to feign a fall.

Rose fell face down into the pond, the glasses came off, the clutch was dropped, and one shoe was lost, then she stood up indignantly, dripping wet. The boys turned around to see what the splash was all about and realised what they had done, but instead of offering to assist, phones and iPads started going off everywhere - exactly as Nic had planned.

Suddenly a hand appeared in front of her as a woman had seen her go in and she wanted to help, but this wasn't in the plan. Rose declined the assistance and started pirouetting along the wall of the cascading water. She was now completely drenched, and in the ever-flowing water, just managed to hear the watch chime at 11.08. Everard was now standing in front of her in the pond. He held out his arm and pulled her from the cascading water. He quickly took off his jacket, guided her into it, and whilst doing up the two buttons whispered; 'Good job.'

Meantime, the BBC boys, and some men, were booing him as he had stopped the show, so Everard had scooped her up in his arms, stepped out of the pond and carried her to the Emergency Exit.

It was now 11.10 and they were behind the wall. Everard nodded to Rose to pull down on the handle, and the alarm started blaring. Museum attendants were coming from everywhere, and Rose knew her role in the plan had worked. They reached the outside exit and Everard set her on her feet. He nodded once again, took his coat, and left her there in the morning sun. He turned and went back inside muttering something that sounded like: 'Good job, Miss Panda-Eyes.'

Rose suddenly realised a flaw in the plan. She had lost her clutch, phone and wallet and did not have any money to get home. A man approached her. 'That's a really good mime. What are you supposed to be, a drowned rat?' He dropped a $20 note at her feet. Rose scooped it up and walked over to the taxi rank. 'I need to go to Hill End Terrace. Not a big job for you, sorry.' Rose quickly stepped into the rear seat.

'Whoa, lady. What have you done? You look like a

panda with those black rings around your eyes. You are still wet. I can't take you.'

Rose held her arms open after being crossed over her chest. The taxi driver saw the movement in his mirror and smiled. 'OK. I'll take you then, Panda-Eyes.'

Rose arrived home, threw the $20 note at the driver and quickly jumped out.

CHAPTER 9

It was now Saturday. Sandy had returned from the sojourn with the Band and they were sitting on the rear deck having breakfast. 'Rose, I know they can make it. They don't fake, it's jazz man, it's the vibe, it's so cool. Sorry, I sound like a band manager already, don't I?' Rose just nodded as they still hadn't heard from Nic and she wondered if the plan failed.

'You still haven't heard from Nic, have you?'

'No.'

'But everything went as planned. I mean you lost your phone, wallet, your shoes, and even my old pair of Buddy Holly glasses. It all went to plan, didn't it?'

'Yes.'

'So, why the blues? Surely you're not stuck on him already. It's only been a total of eight hours that you've known him. I mean, I know there are eight hours in one working day, and some office romances do work, but I can't think of any at the moment.'

'I suppose I could be. I mean it was exciting and scary, but also well-coordinated and very professional. Sorry about your glasses though.'

Sandy smiled. 'Don't worry about it. You did manage to get on telly though. I mean all the Brisbane channels and I even heard it was posted on the net. They are calling you "Miss Panda-Eyes," and one channel even alluded it to as "PandaGOMAeon." You have to admit that's funny.' Rose stifled a laugh and the doorbell rang. Sandy looked up. 'It's Nic.'

'No. I don't know Sandy. I don't know what to think about him just yet.'

'No, it's Nic at the front door. Didn't you say he drives a white Mustang? I think I saw one stop out the front. When did you tell him where we lived?'

'I haven't, but he probably heard it at the will reading.'

Rose made her through the house, and upon opening the front door saw the whole door frame filled with Lisianthus. Nic then peeked out from behind them. 'You know these damn flowers are hard to find in local Brisbane florists. I had to go all the way down to Rocklea Markets for these, and I'm not leaving them in the sink this time either.'

Rose led him out to the back deck and collected a vase along the way. Nic nodded a hello at Sandy. 'Hey, back from the gig? Sticks Out said it went well, and they might get a regular night down there too. Something about you knowing the Booking Agent from when "The She Shed" did events down there.'

'Yes, we still have our contacts, but so do you, Mr Nic Thorn. Sticks told me a lot about you, and your exploits around the place. Here in Brisbane, Adelaide, Melbourne and Perth too. What? Sydney too big for a country boy from Ouyen?'

'Something like that, Sandy. What else did he tell you about me?'

'Well, he said that he'd known you since Churchie's College. You were there together, but he thinks you are a bit older than him. You haven't married yet. You live alone, you like the company of beautiful women, and play a mean lead guitar...mmm... that's about it.'

'So, nothing about my job, then?'

'No, he said that if he did you would hunt him down and kill him. Rose told me that you don't kill people, Nic.'

Nic looked at them and smiled. 'Nope, never, it's not what I do, but I can make an exception right now though.'

'Why?' Rose chimed in.

'Well, I'm sitting on your back deck overlooking the Brisbane River, and neither of you has offered to make me a chai latte.'

Sandy jumped up, saluted, and went into the house. 'Yes sir.'

Rose took a breath and leaned towards Nic. 'Did everything work on Thursday?' Nic grinned. 'Yep, like clockwork, thanks to you and the doppelganger principle. I saw you on TV and the net too. Those downloads translate well to the bigger screen, don't they?'

Rose went to slap him on his arm, but he was too

quick grabbing her hand and folding $500 cash into it. He then presented her with a box containing a new iPhone. The box had already been opened, so she slid the cover and held the new phone in her hand. 'What's the five hundred for? And you bought me a new phone as well?'

'Expenses, Rose. You lost your phone, your clutch, your shoe and your dignity, so five hundred cash, and a new phone might just cover it.'

Rose nodded. 'I did keep some receipts for you if you want them. One from the carpark, and one from the entrance fee into GOMA.'

'Do you have them now?'

'No, they were in my clutch too.'

Nic then presented her with a paper bag. It contained her soggy clutch, soggy wallet, one shoe and her old phone. 'I don't know what happened to the Buddy Holly glasses, or the other shoe. Maybe one of the BBC boys kept them as a memento for the time they met Miss Panda-Eyes at GOMA.'

Rose opened the soggy clutch and peered inside for the receipts. They were soggy too, but she presented them to Nic anyway. 'See I keep my word, and my word is my Bond. I didn't even have to use that, did I?'

'That you didn't, Rose.'

Meantime Sandy came back with tea, saw the new phone on the table, and peered into the paper bag at all the soggy stuff. 'What my Buddy Holly glasses didn't turn up? And what's with the new phone, Rose?

You'll never be able to set it up, neither will I, and we don't know any teenagers. Hang on, the boys from BBC might help.' Sandy moved quickly out of Rose's reach.

Nic smiled. 'The phone is all ready to go. I have a go-to guy who does that stuff, and he recovered enough from your wet phone to transfer the data and contacts over. Hope you don't mind, but you don't have many names in there, do you?'

Rose shrugged. 'Nope, just the important ones. Tell us about the gallery thing.'

'Well, I had my guys dressed the same, and I assume you saw all the Bronco Caps? Well. by the time your little water show was happening, I had my chance to snip the tapestry in four separate places, so the tests could be done on the material. We swapped the jackets inside out, other than that, you know the rest.'

Rose nodded. 'How did you move the camera to get it pointed away?'

'Arguing kids should not be allowed to take helium balloons into galleries, should they? A balloon could cause havoc to the displays, and might even dislodge the view of a camera that might need to be re-set.'

Sandy smiled at the outcome. 'So, was the tapestry a fake?'

'That is the interesting point. No, it wasn't, but the gallery people were very interested in how their systems and safeguards were compromised. It was just a test. They failed, but we didn't.'

Rose nodded. 'Who would try and damage a painting or a tapestry?'

Nic shook his head. 'It's not about that. It's more about the compromising of security systems and protocols.'

Rose nodded again. 'So what's next for us, Nic?'

'Well, I do need an Executive Assistant. Can either of you type?'

Sandy responded to both of them. 'No, but I didn't think we were your type anyway. Sticks Out said that you like to hang out with beautiful women, and we don't think we make the grade.'

Nic shook his head. 'Rose, Sandy. You underestimate your powers of persuasion, and beauty is in the eye of the beholder after all, besides that, I can't find the Buddy Holly glasses anywhere.'

Rose sighed. 'Seriously, Nic, is this the beginning of the end? Or do you have something else in mind for us already?'

'Actually, I do need an Executive Assistant, and it doesn't matter if you can't type. I just need one of you to create a diversion.'

Rose shook her head. 'Where Nic? We can't go back to the gallery, or anywhere near the Performing Arts Centre that's next door either.'

'Nup, this one is in Adelaide.' Rose and Sandy looked at him, then at each other. 'How is that going to work? Can you afford both of us? Don't you have any Minions, in their little blue overalls, working for you?'

Nic was about to respond but yelled out instead. 'Cripes, what is that? Something very large and very fluffy has just come up the stairs. It looks like an eight-kilo wolf in cat's clothing.'

'That's Dog', and Rose leant down to pat the animal on the head. Nic nodded. 'It is a cat isn't it?'

'Yes, a Maine Coon. Sandy and I couldn't agree to get a cat or a dog. When we saw this big thing at the animal shelter, we had to take it home with us. So we called it Dog. It doesn't just catch the mice, as it scares the crap out of them too.'

The cat jumped up onto Nic's lap, proceeded to turn in circles, and then started purring. It was very loud. 'I think someone has stolen the keys to my Mustang, and just started it up.' Sandy laughed. 'Wait until you see our Siberian husky. We call it Catherine, Cat for short.'

'You're kidding right?'

Rose grinned. 'No. It's just you are so easy to tease. OK, tell us about Adelaide.'

'There are two parts. The first one involves falsified invoices and is quite a common scam. Your supplier sends you an invoice, you recognize it and pay within the normal terms, and the perps learn your shipping and payment process - let's use 'The She Shed' as an example. They watch for when you get a delivery, come into the store and wait until the box is opened, then take a photo of the invoice, or take the whole document, and one of your business cards with your email address on it. They send you an email a couple of days later: *"Dear Sandy and Rose, it is always a pleasure doing business with you...blah, blah...and by the way we have changed Banks, we are no longer with ABC Bank, and now are with DEF Bank, so you will receive an amended Invoice with a new Account number"*. You think nothing more of it until a week later you get the amended invoice. It looks the same apart from the change in account details, and you don't check with the Supplier, or even notice that the email had not come from your supplier. Then they remind you to ensure you change the account details in your Internet Banking or whatever, so you make the payment to them instead of the supplier. It's the modern version of stealing a cheque from the mail. Your supplier chases you, and you refer back to the email, "What email?"...

Rose shook her head. 'The money has to go to a bank, Nic. Don't the Banks have a hundred-point identification process and verification stuff to stop this type of thing from happening?'

'Yep, but if the perps are stealing people's identification, driver's licenses etc, it might allow them to open an online account, then the accounts are closed. Until the Banks start taking these types of frauds seriously, it is a fairly simple scam.'

Rose nodded. 'So, why to Adelaide?'

'We are using the Adelaide Motor Show as the main event, offering Hummers to entice them to take the bait.'

They nodded. 'OK, think we got it. So what's number two?'

Nic nodded. 'Much simpler. It's about an investigation into cross-state bottles and cans recycling.'

Rose said she would think about it, but it was a definite 'no' by Sandy as she had left a bad relationship in the rearview mirror of Adelaide a long time ago, and had no intention of ever going back. Nic stood, pushed Dog off his lap, and said he would be back in touch.

CHAPTER 10

They were still trying to work out the ins and outs of it when Rose's phone rang -it was Dimond, and the phone was on speaker as they had been playing with the settings.

Dimond blurted out 'I have left him,' without even saying who it was. 'I mean, he is a jerk. I mean, you saw how he behaved at the will reading. You should have heard him afterwards. I mean, we were standing on the promenade just under Georges Restaurant. I mean, I hope no one heard what he said about the girls, and he still wanted to keep his little shiny new car. He even refused to take it back, I mean.'

Sandy leaned forward. 'Do you think she is going to take a breath, Rose?'

They heard a door slam out the front. 'Where are you, Dimond?'

'Your place. Out the front.'

'How did you know where we lived?'

'Michael told me.'

Rose and Sandy went down the back steps and watched as Dimond was trying to wrangle a bottle of

Bundaberg Rum and two, 2-litre bottles of Coca-Cola. She dropped one of the bottles on the ground and it bounced away, so she took after it - then she tripped on the gutter, fell onto the grassy footpath, and rolled over to face up to the sky.

Rose and Sandy did their best to stop laughing.

'I can hear you two laughing at me. It's not funny. I mean it is funny, but it's not, so stop laughing.'

Sandy whispered to Rose. 'Do you think she has been drinking and driving?'

Dimond called out. 'I heard that. I took a taxi.' Dimond picked herself up, brushed herself down, and looked up as they approached. 'I see you have lost your Panda-Eyes, Rose.' Then she slumped back to the grass, unscrewed the top off the rum bottle, took a big swig neat, followed it with a big gulp of coke, and then burped loudly.

Sandy stifled a laugh. 'Choice Rose, fifteen thousand dollars a term at Saint Margaret's, and she still can't hold her liquor.'

Dimond rolled over. 'It's not the liquor that you have to watch out for Sandy - everyone knows it's the coke, at least that's what we learnt in our drug awareness sessions.'

Rose and Sandy helped her up and noticed Dimond had already consumed about a third of the Bundy bottle, so they separated it from her and then led her to the house and up the rear stairs.

Dimond plonked herself into the Papasan and

promptly shut her eyes. 'Oh, this is nice. Three besties having a drink together. I miss my friends. I mean Michael will let me have friends, but I can't do that until I can find ones that are not as pretty as me. I do have my standards you know, and he has a wandering eye too. Yes, it's true. One eye wanders to the left, and the other to the right, at the same time.'

Rose shook her head. 'Dimond, it's only three in the afternoon, so we think it is a bit early for us to join you if that's OK.'

'Crap, I forgot. I can't start drinking until after I pick up the children. Who is going to pick up the children? I mean, I can't now as I have had a tiny weensy little bit to drink haven't I?' And she let out another loud burp. 'Hey guys, would you guys be able to pick them up for me? You know they go to St Margaret's too. That's where we went wasn't it sister Rose, Rosie, Rosemary? You know Michael sometimes looks at our old school photos, and gets me to dress up as Rhianna, like you used to at school, Rose.' She burped again. 'Oops'.

'I was only fifteen....that's creepy Dimond.'

'Yes, that's true too, and that is what I call him when I get cross at him. My-creep. Get it Mike-Creep?' Dimond still had not opened her eyes.

Rose shook her head. 'I think we do Dimond, but we're not going to collect Skye and Lucy without signed permission from you and Michael. The school has rules to stop that.' Rose leaned to Sandy and whispered. 'Would that still be the case?'

'No idea, but it sounds good. I think we will have to call Michael. Do you still have his number?'

Rose shook her head again. 'Me, no, I deleted it on the day after I divorced him. Actually, it might have been on the day I married him.'

Dimond opened her eyes from her stupor and rocked back in the chair. 'Whoa, who put the rummy in my tummy? And what have you ladies been whispering about? Was it me? Was it that I picked up Michael on the rebound? Was it that I have two lovely children and you don't? Was it that they might not be Michael's? Was it that I am about to be sick?' Dimond jumped up and ran into the house.

'Second door on the right, Dimond, second door.'

She made it, and they waited and waited, and waited. Eventually, she came out. Rose stood up. 'We thought we'd lost you down the plug-hole or something'

'No. Michael rang when I was in there and told me he was sorry. I listened, and think I'll give him a second chance.' They both looked at her. 'Well, maybe it is his sixth or seventh then.'

There was a toot out the front of their place, and Sandy looked around the side of the house. It was Michael. He was in an old Camry. It was beige. He stepped out of the car and had Skye and Lucy in tow. The two young girls scampered down the side of the house, went straight up to Dimond, and hugged her. Michael stayed by the car.

Sandy yelled out to him. 'Nic is not around Michael.' Rose whispered. 'That's nasty Sandy.'

Then they both looked at Dimond as she appeared to be instantly sober. 'Thanks for the chat ladies. We should do this more often. We could do a girl's night out and everything.' Dimond, Lucy and Skye descended the stairs, making their way back to the car with a few out-cries of "whoops-a-daisy" back to Michael and the car.

Michael still had not said a word, but just as the car drove away. Dog suddenly ran over from Dave's place next door, and scared the crap out of Dimond who was leaning out of the passenger window, breathing deeply, and trying to hold it all together.

Sandy noticed and called out 'On ya Dog', then looked at Rose. So married with children? What do you think of it?'

'I think the best thing about married with children was Frank Sinatra's theme song, 'Love and Marriage."

Sandy smiled. 'That's not what I meant and you know it. I mean we are not getting any younger. The big three-0 is looming large for both of us in the headlights, and all that stuff.'

'What's brought this on, Sandy?'

'Well, Michael and Dimond and those little girls. Don't you think it would be you know?' Rose shrugged.

'On that note, I think we should talk some more about Adelaide and Nic, instead of all that, Sandy.'

'OK. I'll grab the Chardy and a couple of glasses. Let's forget about Adelaide for the moment, and just talk about Nic.'

Rose nodded. 'I'll drink to that, and to the fact we didn't tell Dimond that we overheard Michael being a jerk.'

Sandy grinned. 'I agree, so maybe we should have a toast just to us?'

Rose returned, poured the Chardonnay into the glasses, looked at them, decided they were too small, went back inside and grabbed a couple of large brandy balloons instead. Then she emptied half of the bottle into each glass, looked at them, and decided it was too much after all. So, returned inside for an ice bucket and dropped the bottle into the ice, eventually they raised their glasses.

'Here's to Nic. How long has it been now, Rose?'

'Including the hour and a half he was here today, nine and a half hours.'

'So you are not including the thing at GOMA?'

'Nope. I didn't see him there.'

'Oh, he saw you. He told me.'

'Where?'

'At GOMA, he said.'

'No way. I would have recognized him.'

'Remember the man that dropped the twenty dollars at your feet, outside the Emergency Exit door?'

'You're kidding. That was Nic?'

'No, he was the taxi driver that took you home.' Rose considered the comment and then realised she didn't mention what number Hill End Terrace, just the street name.

'Damn you, Nic.'

CHAPTER 11

Later that afternoon, they were gathered around a table at one of the local restaurants. Nic began to read the menu. 'So guys, you want to know more about Adelaide then?' Sandy leaned forward as she thought there was no way he knew about this little gem at the top of Hardgrave Road, West End. 'Yes, but first Nic, have you eaten dinner here at Caravanserai before?'

'No, but I have had lunch here.' Sandy continued: 'Let me guess - they do a great Chai Latte, followed by turkey with cranberry on rye?'

'Nope. I come for the Turkish lemonade - on a hot and muggy Brisbane summer day, they are to die for.' Sandy grinned. 'You say that a lot, Nic'.

'What's that?'

'To die for... would you die for us, Nic?'

'Whoa, Sandy, that's a bit heavy, isn't it? What brought that on?'

"Rose is seriously considering going to Adelaide, so we want to know how dangerous it is going to be. What's the likelihood that she could get into a position where she feels threatened or worse? This is serious Nic. We hardly know anything about you. You could be a mass murderer when it comes down to it.'

Nic nodded. 'OK, the message is coming in loud and clear. I tell you what, let me call someone and if you are happy with what he has to say about me, then we can talk some more.' Nic stood up and walked away from the table to make the call.

Rose watched him. 'It's after seven p.m., and I suspect no one will take a business call that late. I bet when he comes back and says that the person he was trying to call is unavailable at the moment. I'll put a twenty on it.'

Nic came back and Rose was correct - he explained that the man was not currently available, but would ring back. Rose pulled open her purse and handed over the twenty. Nic saw what was going on. 'What, did someone lose a bet about me?'

Sandy sighed. 'Yes, you did. Rose knew exactly what you would say *"I'm sorry, Mr Whoever is not available, but will ring back later."* It cost me twenty, but it was worth it. I can't do this Nic, it is just not... I mean we don't have much going on in Brisbane, but it is our not much going on.'

'So, no convincing you then?' Nic held up his phone and scrolled through the contact list. It was extensive. Most of them had 'called barred' but they recognized a couple of Premiers, Annastacia Palaszczuk (QLD), Steven Marshall (SA), various state politicians, and even some Police Commissioners.

Rose gasped when she saw the name, C Palmer.

Nic waved the phone at them. 'Choose someone that you want to call, anyone at random.'

Sandy nodded. 'OK, but this could all be a setup. The numbers could be faked, and the people answering could be faked. This all sounds like what you do anyway.'

'Good point Sandy. Tell you what, choose the name and we will do it your way. Make it someone contactable, and I'll use your phone to go to a website. We will get through to them that way.'

Sandy grinned. 'Make it the South Australian Police Commissioner, Gerard Steldons, seeing you'd like Rose to go Adelaide. Let's ring him and see what he has to say.'

Nic nodded. 'Interesting, as I was just trying to call him.' They both looked at him suspiciously, then Nic leaned forward. 'Can I use your phone then, Sandy?'

'Sure, but it is locked and you have to guess the password. I will give you a hint, it is three letters and five numbers. The letters are at the start.'

Nic took the phone, looked at Sandy, looked at Rose, tapped the numbers on the screen and it unlocked. 'TSS31513.' Good password Sandy. No one would guess that randomly unless they knew you.'

Rose looked over to Sandy, then to Nic. 'I don't get it, Sandy, what is that?'

Sandy sighed. '"The She Shed.' We opened it on the

31st May 2013, 'TSS31513,' and crap, as that means I have to change my password.'

Sandy looked at him. 'How did you know?'

'I didn't. I guessed it. It was the same password that I was thinking I would set on Rose's new phone, but I left it unlocked. I was going to use 87731513 and not the TSS.'

Nic then scrolled to the SAPOL Office site via www.sapol@sa.gov.au and pressed the contact link, it brought up the sacommisioner@sa.gov.au email address. He filled out his name, his email address, but held the phone away from them when he typed the message and offered an explanation. 'If you see what I typed in there, it won't be me that comes looking for you, sorry about that. The message was sent. They waited, but nothing happened.

Nic took a sip of his lemonade. 'Still don't believe me do you? I tell you what, if Gerard Steldons does not ring back at eight, I'll walk away and you won't see me again. It'll be my loss as I like you guys. If he does, dinner is on me, and Rose is coming to Adelaide. And Sandy, I know you don't want to come, but you can fly down too and stay overnight. I'll put you on the next plane back if you want, so at least you can check everything out.'

Their dinner arrived, and the closer it got to 8, both Rose and Sandy found they had lost their appetites. The drinks came and went, dessert offers came and went, and all the while Nic had not given anything away. He just kept eating and drinking the Turkish lemonade.

It was now eight.

Sandy looked at Rose. Nic looked at his phone, and it rang: 'Yes Gerry, thanks for calling. I am just setting things up now and I'll be down in a few days. I'll catch up with you and the Team on Wednesday at fourteen hundred. Yes, your office this time. Angas Street.' Nic disconnected the call. 'Well, he rang back.'

They looked at him and shook their heads, and Sandy sighed. 'That was lame Nic. We have no idea who you spoke to, or even if there was anyone on the other end of the phone.'

Nic shook his head. 'Wow, you guys are worse than the Spanish Inquisition, and no one expects the Spanish Inquisition.'

Sandy looked at him. 'What's that supposed to mean?'

Nic leaned forward. 'It's from Monty Python Sandy. You know John Cleese, Eric Idle, Michael Palin, those guys. Life of Brian, The Holy Grail?'

Sandy shook her head. 'Were you trying to be funny or something else?'

Rose chipped in trying to relieve the tension 'Yes, it is funny Sandy, and they were probably the best comedy troupe that we'll see in our lifetime. Oh, but there was the Goodies, and the Two Ronnies.'

Nic grinned. 'Wow Rose, I didn't know that you

had a sense of humour. Oh, that didn't come out like it was supposed to, did it?'

Rose smiled. 'Not exactly, but you have seen my silly walk.'

'True. It was silly, and a good walk too.'

Sandy looked at them. 'What the hell are you two talking about?'

Nic sighed. 'Never mind, Sandy, but what is next from here? I mean I can give Mr Steldons a call back now, but I am meeting with him in two weeks and the offer is still there for both of you. So, please think about it, and I'll call back at your place for a decision on Monday. That gives you a week to think about it.'

Rose nodded. 'Thanks, Nic. See you then.'

Nic stood up. 'I've got the tab already, so it's good-night from me.' Rose quipped back quickly. 'And it's goodnight from him.'

They watched him walk away, and this time he turned back and smiled.

'How did he do that again Rose? I mean, how did he know how much the bill was going to be, and pay for it up front?'

Rose nodded. 'It was a set menu and a set price, including the Turkish lemonades, not that clever.'

'OK, but what about the other day when he turned up at our place? You hadn't told him where we lived and neither had I?'

'At the will reading our addresses were read out.'

'So, that explains how Dimond knew where we lived. It wasn't Michael then?'

'I hope not.'

'OK, I'll give you that one, but how did he know our mobile numbers?'

Rose sighed. 'Well, that one I am still trying to work out.'

Whilst they were standing there, a sleek black 300C Chrysler pulled up to the kerb, and they looked at it. The darkened passenger side window slid down and a voice came from within, most likely from the driver's side as there was no one in the passenger seat.

'Y'all mighty fine ladies should not be out alone on a night like this. Hop in and I will take you for a ride;' a voice came forth with a Southern American drawl.

Rose stepped back. 'Nope, we are good thanks. We're just waiting for a taxi.'

The car didn't move, the window went up, and this time the back side window came down instead, and another voice came from within.

'Whoa, lady. What have you done? You look like a panda. You are still wet. I can still take you though."

'Damn you, Nic.'

They stepped in and he drove them home.

CHAPTER 12

'Everything is a drag isn't it, Rose? I mean it's been a while since we've had something exciting to do, and this Nic guy seems to be offering it in spades. So, why are we still so ...well, hung up about not getting involved?'

Rose sighed. 'At least it's Monday now, and we should be hearing from him today.'

Sandy shrugged. 'He hasn't rung you or anything since the dinner then?'

'No. I think I would like to get more involved with him, but am not sure I want to get involved in the things that he gets involved in.'

'Wow. OK, I think I get it.'

The doorbell rang, and Rose stood up. 'I didn't hear a car?'

'Me either.' Rose went through the house this time and opened the door. It was Nic. He was dressed in a half wetsuit, had a beer in one hand, and a life jacket in the other. The wetsuit was open and unzipped down to his waist. It was tight against his chest and his arms were exposed. Rose didn't know where to look, so she tried his eyes and thought they were like big pools of dark chocolate.

He saw her looking him over and smiled. 'Have you ever been on a skiff, Rose? It's such a rush. I mean they told me the bay off Wynnum is good, but you have to tack so much more when you are on the river, you don't even have the time to take a breath.'

Rose tried to avert her gaze from his eyes. 'You're still wet....Mr. ...um... "Mr Bright as a Button" - come in and get changed. You do have something else to change into, don't you?'

Sandy had now come to the door and saw it was Nic. 'Nice.'

'Hi Sandy, and yep, clothes in my backpack.'

They showed him to the spare room to get changed and pointed to the adjoining bathroom. Nic eventually came out and joined them on the rear deck. He was towel-drying his hair. 'Best thing ever guys, a hot shower after a couple of hours sailing.'

'Surely it's not the best thing ever, there might be a couple of other things that are up there too.' Sandy moved out of the way trying to avoid a slap from Rose.

'So tell me, guys. What's the decision about Adelaide?'

Rose nodded. 'We're both in.'

'OK great. I'll get my team to send you the itinerary, and thanks again. It won't be as exciting as Uncle Albert's funeral, but Adelaide does have its wineries and churches. If you hate it all, you can always drink too much, and fall asleep in the confessional.'

Rose shrugged. 'I don't think we'll be able to be drinking or sleeping at all with you in the same room with us. You might snore after all.'

Nic nodded. 'I've thought about that too, and have to burst your bubble right there. We won't be in the same room, in fact, we won't even be in the same hotel.'

Sandy sighed. 'What? Why?'

'Disappointing I know, it's all about the image. Gone are the days when you would bring your EA to a function, in this case, two EAs, and have them stay anywhere near you.'

'How is that going to work then, Nic?'

'Well, I will be at the Intercontinental, which is next to the Adelaide Convention Centre, where the show is, and you two will be across the road at the Stamford Plaza. Oh, hang on, as you are coming as my superiors, it will be the other way around. Hope you enjoy five stars, whilst I'm slumming across the road.'

Sandy grinned. 'The Stamford Plaza is not exactly slumming it Nic. I have stayed there, I used to live in Adelaide.'

Rose interrupted the banter. 'You won't be tempted to cross the road will you Nic, just like that crazy chicken? I mean why *did* the rooster cross the road? To get to the chicks on the other side of course.'

'Hey, that's funny Rose. You do have a sense of humour in there somewhere don't you?'

'Cluck, cluck, Nic. Anyway, what is this all about, and why is Commissioner Steldons involved? Are you Batman in disguise?'

Nic grinned. 'That would be Commissioner *Gordon* if I was Batman. I assume you checked that Gerard Steldons' middle name is not Gordon.'

Rose nodded. 'So, what's your role?'

'Well, I am the bait. Well, we will be. I'm going to have access to ex-US Army Hummers that are becoming available, about five of them, with access to another ten. The cost will be around seventy grand each. Anyone in the industry knows security protocols for handling the sale of government assets are rumoured to be a bit, well lazy, for want of a better word.'

Sandy nodded. 'Those damn Yank Tanks - over here and oversized.'

'Not quite Sandy, but never mind. Anyhow, so together with the assistance of the South Australian Police, we're going to attract the big fat stupid bees, to the big fat pot of money, honey.'

Sandy nodded. 'This sounds a bit dangerous, Nic.'

Nic shook his head. 'It's all about the paper trail rather than the people involved, so, it's all about the image. We need to appear to be as naïve as we can and portray that we can't possibly be scammed. It might just work.'

Rose nodded. 'You're still talking about 'we.' Nic how can we, be we?'

Nic grinned. 'That's the point. Rose, if you are both coming, one of you can be my boss, or both of you can.'

Rose smiled. 'Oh, does that mean that we will have the power to do what we say?'

'Yep, something like that, and who knows you may even like it. You'll both be in character and need to pretend to be arrogant the whole time. If everything goes to plan, the queen or king bee, as we don't know who is behind it as yet, will turn up and make their play. The joint venture between SAPOL and Victorian Police had been tracking the scammers from over in Melbourne. The group recently left Geelong, and bobbed up again in Mount Gambier at a 'Show & Shine' so it's presumed they were heading into Adelaide for the motor show.'

Sandy nodded this time. 'Tell us about the other thing then, the re-cycling scam. Is that still going on?'

"Yep. Word has got around that there is a shipment of bottles and cans that keep coming into South Australia, from over the border. They get trucked into Adelaide, and claim the refund on bottles not purchased there.'

'That doesn't sound like a such big deal, Nic.'

'It still is, Rose. It involves the government paying out some money that they should not have to.' Rose nodded. 'And that's a SAPOL matter too?'

'Actually, it's the Environment Protection Authority that ante up the refunds.'

'So, what's the fine – a slap on the wrist?'

'Nup, if it's proven to be a commercial venture by a registered business, the fine can be up to five grand, per event for the scam. That's why we are down here for ten days as we'll be taking a drive to Pinnaroo, as it's where they think the truck might be crossing the border.'

Rose nodded again. 'Sounds good then, but what do we need to pack? How many outfits? How many pairs of shoes? How much spending money do we get in case the weather changes and we don't have anything to wear?'

Nic leant down to pat the cat. 'Wow, it was so much easier when I used to bring my twin sister along to these things.'

Sandy looked at him. 'You have a twin sister, and never told us? Tell us about her. Where does she live? And can we get her to come along too? We could be Nicky's Angels if there were three of us.'

'She married a farmer from Murrayville and no, she won't be coming along, and no, you won't ever get to meet her. Family protection and all that.'

'Will you at least tell us her name? You know, just in case we meet her in downtown Murrayville when we are doing some grocery shopping and we don't want to be rude?'

'OK.. it's....it's...never mind. I'm not falling for this.

You could track her down in the phone book, and I don't want you ringing her, and talking girly stuff about me.'

Rose sighed. 'Nic, that's so disappointing.'

Nic continued: 'In two days, please meet with me at Brisbane Airport. We'll be flying QANTAS. Everything will be in play. Oh, and dress like you are tough, no-nonsense businesswomen that don't take crap from any man, breaching the glass ceiling and all.'

Rose looked at him. 'Just how do we dress like that?'

'I'm sure you will work it out, and bring along at least two suitcases and carry-on for the trip, to look the part.'

Rose and Sandy were waiting inside the Brisbane Airport and wondering again if it was all another set-up, but Nic had texted them that he was running a little late, and when they finally saw him were shocked by the vision. He was completely dishevelled, had a grungy old brown leather bag over one shoulder, a large duffel bag on his back, and trailing behind was a solid computer bag. All of it looked very unlike him.

Nic approached them, grimaced, then whispered, 'How do you like this get up? I am still Nic but my surname is Thyme, and both of you in your roles always refer to me as Nick-o-las with the pauses. never Nic.'

'Yes, I think we got it, and by the way Nick-o-las, can you get our bags.'

Nic laughed, and then went straight into the role

play, commanding loudly but politely. 'Please both leave all your bags here and I will attend to them. I have your tickets here in my pocket. You can make your way straight through the scanners, and to the QANTAS Lounge as normal. Here are your QANTAS Cards. I will collect you when the flight is announced.'

Rose looked at him, at Sandy, and then whispered; 'Don't we get new names too, Nick-o-las?'

'Yes. Please check that I have given you the correct boarding passes. We are departing in twenty minutes.'

Rose looked at her card, showed Sandy and then looked at Nic. 'You're kidding, right? I am Rosie Rhynge?'

Nic smiled and whispered. 'A tissue, a tissue, we all fall down.'

Sandy turned her card over and read it aloud. 'Sandy Olsson - that's a nice name, Nic.'

Nic whispered to her. 'Tell me about it stud.' He walked away and corralled a couple of trolleys, then another man suddenly appeared to assist him with the luggage.

Rose and Sandy went straight through the scanners, up to the lounge, and after forty-five minutes, two Chardonnay's and a couple of chilled olives later, a QANTAS attendant approached them to advise an escort was waiting at the front desk.

Meantime Rose had explained to Sandy that the name 'Olsson' was Olivia Newton-John's character from Grease, however, Rose was still annoyed with

Nic, as her surname 'Rhynge' read with the names around the other way, made her 'Rhynge Rosie.' Sandy looked at the QANTAS Card. "I still don't get it, Rose, sorry 'Rosie.' What's wrong with Rhynge?'

Rose sighed. 'Pronounced with a Nordic sound, it becomes 'Rhynga.' Nic has named me 'Ringa Rosie'. Damn you Nic, 'Nick-o-las.'

Nic finally met them at the QANTAS counter, and he looked the same as they had seen him in the foyer when they arrived. Sandy grinned. 'You do the stressed out, 'man I don't want to be here' look so well Nic. I bet it is the same look you will have after we have hit the shops in Adelaide for an afternoon too.'

Nic shrugged. 'Remember it's Nick-o-las, and it is time to go ladies.'

Upon boarding, he left them in Business Class, and they watched him go down the middle aisle. Rose commented that she bet he was sitting amongst the unaccompanied children at the back of the plane. 'Make it a twenty and you're on, Rose. Surely he wouldn't do that to himself.' They sat down, sipped on the now-delivered glass of Riesling, and both smiled at the thought.

The flight was uneventful, and two hours, and twenty minutes later, the plane was taxiing down the pale grey tarmac at the sunny Adelaide Airport. They disembarked and waited for him, finally gave up, then stopped along the way at the Haigh's Chocolate outlet for a bag full of 'stress busters'.

Upon leaving the shop, heard their names being called, and when they turned saw Nic chasing up behind them. The front of his shirt was wet. 'I'm very sorry ladies. I was allocated to sit between two young girls, neither had travelled before, and they hadn't taken any air sickness tablets either.'

Rose handed over the twenty dollars, and then Nic moved closer and whispered. 'Let's get this show on the road.'

The group made their way down the escalators. Nic directed them to take a seat whilst he organised the collection of the luggage and the car. Sandy grinned. 'I could get used to this, being waited on by men, Rosie.'

The same man, who had assisted Nic in Brisbane collected the luggage and approached them. 'I'll be collecting the car and meeting you outside by the taxi rank. Please make your way over there. I'll take around twenty minutes, and we will be waiting there for you.'

Rose nodded. 'Do you have a name?'

'Yes. Driver.'

'OK, do you have a first name?'

'No.'

Rose nodded. 'Is that as in Dr No, the Bond villain?' He leaned very closely toward Rose and Sandy, and his scent was Brut aftershave.

'No, it's just Driver. Nic warned me about you two, so behave.'

They watched as Driver and Nic went off with the luggage to collect the car, and walked over to the taxi rank wondering what type of car they would be in. The endless line of yellow and white taxis passed them and they hoped it wouldn't be something little and squeaky.

'They will collect us in a Hummer won't they, duh-ling, Rosie?'

Rose looked at Sandy 'What's with the posh English voice all of a sudden? I don't think you will be able to carry that off for ten days. What if you meet someone you know? What are you going to say then? Sorry, I am talking with the silly English lilt as I have a cold?'

'Good point, thanks, Rosie.'

Nic was now coming towards them. 'I am sorry ladies. Sorry to keep you waiting, but our Driver instructed you to wait in the wrong place. You needed to be around here to the left, not at the taxi rank. I am so sorry.'

Rose leaned into Sandy. 'He is acting, right? I mean he looks like he's overacting, but he could still be acting couldn't he?'

Nic heard the comment and winked.

Sandy stepped back. 'Does he do that a lot, Rosie? It was a bit creepy.'

Rose nodded. 'Not often, but he does have a fascination with my nose.'

Nic beckoned them to follow, and they proceeded around the corner to where Driver was waiting next to a bright white Statesman Caprice. He was now dressed as a professional driver and even had a flat black cap and matching black leather gloves. Just as he opened the doors for them, Sandra loudly castigated him for making them wait and for wasting their time.

Driver looked at her without a reaction, shut the door behind her, and walked Rose around to the other side. Nic sat in the front passenger seat and they were in the rear. Nic turned to Sandra and asked her what that was all about.

Sandy shrugged. 'I was acting Nic. I mean, we have to be mean. You told us it would be OK if were mean to you. I thought it was good to practice, didn't you Rosie?'

Rose shook her head. 'A bit early don't you think, Sandra?'

Nic nodded. 'Probably, but now that you have got that out of the way, it's all about the look, not the words. I don't need either of you to say very much at all while you are on show. I just need you to be seen to be annoyed about anything, and not let it be known by saying anything. Make sense?'

'Mm" and "Mm" they responded with.

Driver shook his head, then leant over to Nic. 'Hey Nic, it's not too late to put them on the last plane back to Brisbane, tonight is it?'

'Sorry mate, it is, unfortunately.'

As they were motoring along Sir Donald Bradman Drive, Sandy began to cry. 'Nic I have missed Adelaide. I didn't think I did but ...' Rose held her hand then called out. 'Please stop the car, Driver.' but he ignored her. Nic turned around to find out what was going on, saw Sandy facing out the window, and noticed that she was crying.

'What's up Sandra Dee, was it in Adelaide that you lost your virgin...?' But before he could finish Sandy looked at him. 'I said I never wanted to come back here. Damn it Nic, why don't you listen?'

Nic nodded. 'Take a left here please, Driver.'

They pulled into the carpark at the back of a Hotel. Driver stopped the car and turned off the engine. Rose opened her door, stepped out, and moved around the other side to Sandy, who had already stepped out. Rose opened Nic's door. 'Please let me get this.' Nic nodded, and Rose moved Sandy away from the car.

'What's up, Sandy? Breathe.'

'It's been a long time since I left, and thought I could cope, but it's so real now. I am here, and I don't know if I can do it. It was so ugly and brutal. I thought it was love, but then it wasn't, and then it got nasty and I got out. I lost everything here. I was ...I almost lost my life too. Then I went back to Brisbane, found you and Uncle Albert, and started again. I found my-self in Brisbane, and you made it all possible.'

Rose softly rubbed her forearm. 'You haven't told me much about what happened. I can't even under-stand all that you went through, but you are here with me and we can...well, just be us here and now and see that lump of a guy in the car? Not just the one in the driver's seat, but the other one too. They are here, and we are here, and we are all together.'

Sandy sniffed. "That's a line from a Beatles song. You know that don't you?'

'No, sorry Sandy I don't. Which one?'

'I am the Walrus.'

Rose nodded. 'OK, I'll call you a Walrus if it keeps you happy.'

Sandy smiled. 'No ...it's, oh never mind.'

Rose and Sandy hugged and stepped into the car.

Nic turned to them. 'So, are we good?'

Rose nodded. 'Yes, but can you do us a favour? If Sandy needs to go back home, like really quickly, can we work with that and let her go?'

Nic nodded. 'Yep, absolutely, and here take these too.' Nic handed them each a Credit Card. 'You'll be able to use these whilst we are here and go if you need to go, Sandy. Meantime use these as you think is necessary.'

Sandy smiled. 'For anything we want, Nic?'

Nic nodded again. 'Yep, just make sure it relates to the job, and of course, get a receipt, so I can do an audit of our trip's expenses when we get back.' With that comment, Driver stifled a laugh. 'Good one Nic, since when do you do any paperwork?'

Nic shrugged. 'As of right now, after all, I am their EA aren't I?'

Sandy had settled down a bit by now. 'Did you happen to notice the name of the Hotel, Rose?'

Rose nodded. 'Yes, it was the Hilton. That's certainly down-market for that group, isn't it? I mean it was only one storey and all. More like a pub.'

Sandy grinned. 'Rose, it's not *the* Hilton Hotel, as that one is in the CBD. This is the Hilton Hotel in Hilton, the suburb' Rose nodded. 'It must be confusing for people coming into Adelaide for the first time.'

CHAPTER 13

They drove into the city, took a left onto King William Street, another left onto North Terrace and Driver pulled into the Stamford Plaza drop-off. Nic stepped out and took his luggage from the boot. 'Give me about ten minutes to check in, and take stuff to my room.' He was back in less than five instead.

'I am terribly sorry ladies. I forgot my manners. I must always have your importance considered over my own. Driver, please take the ladies immediately to their hotel.'

Sandy leaned into Rose. 'He is acting again, isn't he? I mean I can tell, as his left eye starts to twitch.'

'I heard that Sandy, and it is not a twitch. It's a tic, so stop making fun of it.'

Driver moved out of the circular driveway and took a left and an immediate right when Rose and Sandy happened to notice the oncoming tram bearing down on them. Driver called out. 'Oops, sorry, I forgot that Adelaide has trams in North Terrace now.' He accelerated across the tracks and drove up the ramp into the Intercontinental - the two Hotels were almost directly opposite each other. Nic bounded quickly out of the car. Nic moved around to the rear, called over a waiting porter, carefully and very neatly placed the luggage on the trolley, and finally went back to open the rear doors for Sandy and Rose.

All the while Driver hadn't moved out of his seat and leaned back to them. 'It's all part of the show. Everything is his job. Mine is to only drive, and open the doors for you to let you in, never to get out, as it may appear that I'm being impatient with you. So says, Nic.'

Nic politely directed them inside, asked them to take a seat, checked if they would like a drink and were comfortable, and then went up to the reception area. Rose leaned into Sandy this time. 'How long do you think he will put up with having to look out for us? The whole ten days?'

Sandy shook her head. 'Nope, I'll put up a twenty that it will stop once he shows us into our room.'

Rose grinned. 'You're on.'

Nic completed the paperwork, gave the porter a nod and asked them to follow him to the lifts. He also told them they were sharing a twin room due to the Motor Show being next door to their Hotel. When they reached the lifts another couple were waiting, so he apologised to them for being in their way. Rose noticed Nic had raised his hand to his eye.

They took the next elevator and arrived on the 23rd floor. The porter led the way, and using his door pass let them in, then showed them around the room. Nic opened the curtains so they could see the view of Adelaide. The porter left, and Nic flopped down on the nearest bed. 'I'm exhausted already, and it's only been four hours playing this character, and what a wimp he's turned out to be.'

Rose handed over the money. 'Stop your whining, you just cost me a twenty.'

It was now around eight p.m. and not quite dark, so Sandy could point out some of the places of interest from the balcony. 'There's the Myer Centre and David Jones, and that's about all I can remember so far. The Casino is next door, the railway station is underneath us. Rundle Mall is over there, and just across the road there is a really ugly troll named Nick-o-las Thyme.'

'Hey, I resemble that, Sandy.'

'So get out and go back there. Rose and I need some girly time to get all of our girly stuff out of our girly suitcases.'

They started opening their cases, then the drawers and cupboards, looking where to store their clothes. Nic stood up. 'Can't I stay here and watch? I mean my eye is twitching so much at the moment I'll just keep it closed whilst you put all your drawers, well......in the drawers.' They both exclaimed: 'No, Nic, get out.' He grumbled and left.

Sandy folded the last of her clothes into a drawer. 'I lost that bet Rose, and you know I don't think he even noticed I had folded the bathrobe into my suit-case - they are just so plush and warm and everything. Hotel bathrobes are still free for the taking aren't they?' Rose went for a walk around the room. It didn't take long, but then she noticed there was a third door through the cupboards. She tried the lock and it opened into another room. 'I call dibs.'

Sandy moved towards Rose. 'On what?'

Rose smiled. 'Have a look. I mean Nic said it was a twin, but I didn't realise he meant twin rooms.' Rose proceeded to show Sandy the other room through the partitioned door.

They stepped through and it was a complete room with a king-size bed, bathroom, mini-bar, TV and sitting area. It even had a view across the top of Parliament House towards the east.

'I'll pay you twenty dollars if you let me stay in here.'

'I don't think so.'

"OK, how about I give you free rein on my Credit Card?' Sandy handed Rose the Credit Card that Nic had provided for her in the car.

'Still nope.'

Sandy tried again. 'OK, I tell you what, I'll order housekeeping to come up and join my two teeny, tiny single beds together, and hopefully, it will make a bed that is about half the size of the one you have in here.'

Rose nodded. 'I think that will work.'

They went back into the other room and spent some

time discussing who would make the call to Housekeeping. Eventually Rose agreed that she would, as she had known Nic for five hours more than Sandy. 'Rose, you will need to use your officious, no-nonsense voice with them. You know that don't you?'

'Sure, and I've been practicing it. Do you want to hear it?'

Sandy stood back a little. 'Give it to me with all guns blazing. I had better sit down though.'

'Here it comes.....'GOD DAMN YOU NICK-O-LAS, CAN'T YOU UNDERSTAND PLAIN ENGLISH? I SAID I WANTED ENGLISH BREAKFAST, NOT A CHAI LATTE."

'Whoa Rose, where has that big girl voice tone been hiding all your life? I mean I was almost scared, nope, I was scared, and need a drink right now to calm my nerves.' Sandy promptly got up, went to the bar fridge, opened it, popped open the champagne, and took a swig directly from the bottle.

Rose laughed, called Housekeeping (didn't use the big girl voice) and about thirty minutes later they were staring at the new, almost king-sized bed that Sandy would now be sleeping on. Sandy sat down on the bed and was disappointed with its firmness. 'I will make it thirty then. Rose.'

It was morning, around 10 am, and Rose and Sandy had been up for about an hour, still in the suite, fully dressed, and were wondering where Nic was.

Both mobiles were plugged into the chargers (face down to avoid the dreaded blue light that would make their faces go all wrinkly), and in the meantime had started eating through the snacks from the mini-bar for breakfast.

The phone rang in the suite. Sandy answered. It was Nic.

'I am sorry to interrupt you, Sandra. I was wondering where you both were as you have missed our morning's nine a.m. meeting in the breakfast parlour on Level One.'

'You are downstairs aren't you Nic, and there was no nine o'clock was there? So I assume that you are acting. Is your eye twitching yet?'

Nic paused at the other end. 'Oh, that is so nice of you to say that to me. I don't deserve all that praise, but it is honestly appreciated. So thank you.'

Sandy continued. 'What do you want us to do?'

'Thank you for asking. Can you please meet me in the Atrium in thirty minutes, and I'll discuss today's agenda. Does that suit you both?'

Rose called out. 'Not really Nick-o-las, you see, there was a lot of noise coming from an ugly troll at the Stamford Hotel across the road last night. We didn't sleep very well. We both need our beauty sleep you know.'

Nic ignored her comment. 'So, that is good, and thank you for agreeing to meet me. See you both at ten-thirty in the Atrium.'

Sandy hung up the phone. 'Hey Rose, did you know we had a nine o'clock with Nick-o-las?'

'Nope.'

They laughed, then checked their phones, and there were two text messages from Nic. Sandy sighed. 'I guess we didn't think that he would text instead of ringing, how rude.'

They caught the lift downstairs and were both dressed in 'business suits.' Rose wore a dark sea blue suit, and ivory shirt with matching clutch and shoes, whilst Sandy was dressed in a black pencil skirt, ivory silk blouse and small handbag which matched the colour of her pearl drop earrings.

They found Nic and walked over to him. He had his back to them but must have sensed their approach. He turned, smiled, then quickly dropped the admiration, and went back to his stressed-out persona. 'Thank you for coming down, ladies. Driver is waiting for us in the porte-cochere, and we will discuss our agenda once you are comfortable in the car.'

The group moved outside and found Driver waiting by the car and he assisted them to step inside. Nic entered the car once he was satisfied they were both inside. 'Crap, I mean, please beg my pardon. I know you're supposed to be, well, I thought that you both would look good, but I think you'll have to tone down a little, otherwise, we might just scare off the mark.'

Suddenly paparazzi, ran up to the car and camera flashes were going off. Rose and Sandy looked at Nic, and they shielded their faces from the intrusions. Sandy managed to whisper. 'Is this for us?'

Nic shook his head. 'Nup, sorry to disappoint you, but this was Justin Bieber's car. He left yesterday afternoon, and the rumour is that he is still in Adelaide somewhere. Who knew he was so popular? I'll take care of it, but you might have to step out of the car to show them that we are not Beliebers. Best we do it all at the same time, so 1...2...3, go.'

'Baby, baby, baby, oh' Sandy muttered as she opened her door to the waiting throng, and she managed to catch one of the photographers in the side of his head with her door. Rose stepped out too, and a photographer immediately took her picture. She looked at him, he looked at her. 'You're not him.'

'No, I'm not, so get your stupid camera out of my face. We're here for the Motor Show and to sell some ex-US Army Hummers. So, unless you have seventy-grand to spare, move out of the way right now.' Nic looked at her and smiled, then the paparazzi realised the situation and started to walk away.

Driver started the engine and they drove down the ramp into North Terrace. He remained particularly wary of the trams coming from the right and pulled across the road to take a right-hand turn. Fortunately, he saw a tram on his left, but it was stopped at the station. Driver still hesitated, and they were now stopped in the middle of the 'Keep Clear' turning section of the road. A taxi beeped at them, and Sandy gave the finger. Nic called out. 'You know that it is one-way, blackened glass so he wouldn't have seen that.'

'Oh, no I didn't.'

Driver looked over to Nic. 'Sorry mate. I forgot again. It's changed so much since I was last here. I mean they've even demolished Footy Park at West Lakes - it's just a barren waste site now. And what's with the new lights at Adelaide Oval? They must keep all the possums awake at night.'

'Settle down, Driver. Let's talk about it later, but meantime do you think we could move?' Driver completed the turn and they headed west down North Terrace. Sandy piped up from the back seat. 'I remember the stadium at West Lakes They played AFL final matches there. Can we have a look then please, Nic?'

'Sure, Sandy, it's on the way. We're not meeting with the others until one p.m.."

Rose called out 'Others? What others? I thought we were the others?' Nic grinned. 'Not exactly Rose, it takes a lot of planning and professional people to put something as big as this all together. We are due to meet the others at The Grand Hotel in the seaside suburb of Glenelg for a Hummer selling presentation – they will run through it, sell it, and tell us what is going down and how it is going down. Then we have a meeting with Gerard Steldons and his Team at sixteen-hundred in Angas St Police HQ in the CBD, to go over their side of it.'

Rose leaned forward. 'You said it was fourteen

hundred when we hooked this up before, why has it changed Nic? Is there something you are not telling us like it's all a con? Including Driver here?'

'No, guys it's not, but you are still suspicious aren't you? I mean even after you ordered Housekeeping to come and change Sandy's bed into a King and all? Do you still think it's a set-up? I think you should apologise to the Driver too. You might've hurt his feelings.' Driver responded. 'That's fine Nic, I mean these two have been good so far, but they are not as good as your sister Gwen are they?'

Sandy perked up. 'Sister Gwen. Ah Ha, so your sister's name is Gwen. I'm going to googoogalise it straight away. How do you spell Murrayville?'

'Sorry Sandy, it won't be that easy'

'What? Is there a jammery thing in the car, and I won't get a signal?'

'Nup.'

'What then?' Rose quipped quickly, and Nic sighed 'There is a sister Gwen, but she's a nun.' Sandy responded this time. 'Your sister is a nun? That explains a lot about you.'

Driver looked over to Nic as he turned off Port Road towards West Lakes Boulevard. 'Sorry Nic, I didn't mean to start this with them.'

Nic turned around to face them. 'I use different people for different jobs. I once used a nun, her name was Gwen, and that's all it was. Driver worked with her too. We both remember the job well. Don't we Driver?'

'Too well, Nic. I don't think she's quite recovered yet either.' Nic continued: 'Gwen became a little intense during the experience, and when it was over she jumped into the Torrens River off the University Bridge. She was never the same after that - must have swallowed too much of the river water. It was such a shame as I can never use her again. If I need a nun again though, how about one of you? Do either of you live a life of poverty, chastity and obedience?'

Sandy grinned and looked at Rose. 'Us, well no...but two out three ain't bad.'

They arrived at the site that was once the pride of South Australian football. It was now a barren wasteland of weeds, broken cement and building debris. Driver stopped the car and they stepped out. Sandy wanted to go through a split in the fence, but Nic held her back. 'Sorry, but you can't ruin those nice new shoes for this, especially seeing I might have paid for them.'

Sandy stood her ground. 'There has to be something I can take from here. I mean, I don't just want a little bit of rock, but something footy. Maybe Driver could go in and have a look for me?'

Driver shook his head. 'Sorry ma'am, but I do have something in the boot that might do. I'll have a look and you see what you think.' Driver moved around the rear of the car, clicked the remote, and rummaged around a little in the boot. ' Found it...' and he presented his find to Sandy. It was one half of a pair of crocheted baby's socks, in the double blue colours of the SANFL's, Sturt Football Club.

Sandy held it against her chest. 'For me? I don't know what to say, are you sure? I mean where is the other half? Don't you need it? It looks almost new.' Driver shook his head. 'I used the other one to clean the car windows and then threw it away. I lashed out last night and bought a chamois for the windows instead.'

Sandy sighed. 'Look at this Rose, it's my very own footy sock, and it's my team too, the Double Blues. Wow, that was such a long time ago.'

Nic smiled. 'OK Sandy, can we go now?'

'Not yet, please.' Rose and Sandy then went for a walk along the fenced perimeter of the once-proud football site.

Driver lent towards Nic. 'I've got a receipt for the chamois.' Nic smiled. 'Don't worry about it ya big softy, nice touch though, and thanks for researching Sandy to find her favourite SANFL team. I thought she might have liked something nice from Adelaide. After all, she almost lost her life here.'

Driver nodded. 'I hope she doesn't run into her ex whilst she is down here. On second thoughts, I hope that we run into him, just to have a quiet word about life choices.' Nic shook his head. 'Yep, maybe, but we don't know the back story, and in my line of work there is always a back story.'

Rose and Sandy returned from their walk, were

guided back into their seats and were driven further along the road heading for their rendezvous at Glenelg. Sandy pointed out the West Lakes Shopping Centre. 'There are some great dress shops in there.' Nic called out without turning around. 'No, Sandy....we don't have the time.' Driver whispered. 'They talk a lot about old times don't they?'

Nic nodded. 'Yep, and it is true that everything that used to be good in Adelaide is gone, missing or has been sold ever since Victoria stole The Grand Prix in '95.'

'Do tell, O Great Wise One.' came from the back seat.

'Another time, my little Beliebers...another time.'

Driver then motored over to The Grand Hotel and found a park in the basement. The group took an elevator to the second floor where the presentation was to take place. 'Guys, please hide your disappointment as it won't be set up like a Bedouin Tent in there. There might not be a single camel anywhere to be found.'

'Just behave.'

Nic looked around to see which one had commented.

It was Driver.

CHAPTER 14

They were about to go into the conference room when Nic stopped and brought them back to a smaller office. He shut the door and gestured for them to take a seat. Nic remained standing.

Sandy watched him pacing the floor. 'What's up, Nic?'

'It's Nick-o-las, and my surname is Thyme. This will be our first real test. There are people in there that are part of my team and there are people in there that are not. Driver doesn't know who they are either yet, so don't go looking for him if you get stuck. Just behave like you think you know it all, but don't say anything to anyone that might give it away. Just be you, playing the roles.'

Sandy took a breath. 'This is getting serious now, isn't it, Rose?'

'Yes, and I have only had about an hour of exposure to this stuff so far, and look how that turned out - it was all over the net. I am the one & only Miss Panda-Eyes.' Rose stood up and took a bow.

Driver looked at her. 'That was you? Wow, my son

has seen it too. I must tell him I've met Miss Panda-Eyes. He'll be so impressed.'

Nic looked at him, grinned and opened the door. 'Ready, guys?'

Sandy nodded. 'Ready as we will ever be, or never be, whatever will be, will be, I guess.'

Nic looked at Sandy. 'That was Doris Day, not Sandy Olsson, from Grease. Oh, and I have to warn you, don't get too close to the Bird Colonel, he is a bit... well... handsy.'

Sandy and Rose nodded. 'Good tip. Thanks Nick-o-las.'

The room was wall-to-wall geek. Computers were set up in the middle surrounded by ear-podded youths. Tables full of finger food, and another full table of wine. There was also a pile of boxes covered by a large camouflage net. The biggest display was at the opposite end of the room though. A giant U-shaped TV screen shrouded by a black curtain was showing a real-time view, looking out the windows of an ex-US Army Hummer. The Hummer was in full motion.

Over to the western side, was a glorious view of the Glenelg beach and beyond to the gulf. Over to the left, was the only other woman in the room. She was giving a PowerPoint presentation to a small group of army personnel and a couple of other men. They seemed to be more fixated with the sleek dark blue power suit that she was wearing, rather than the topic itself. She was early 20's and seemed to have them all under her spell.

Rose and Sandy took it all in, then they noticed a small stage off to the left.

Nic nodded at them. 'If you care to make your way up to the stage and take a seat, I'll be up there soon too.' Then he realised his mistake and began to lead them there. He lightly took their hands, led them up the stairs, sat them down and fussed around them a little, then subtlety pointed out the Colonel. 'The Colonel is one of the 'money men' for all of this, so be careful.'

Meantime, the Colonel had seen the two ladies on the stage and was now heading straight for them. He attempted to make the small jump onto the stage, but his timing was off and stumbled instead. Rose saw him falling and went to assist, but quickly Nic whispered, 'Don't, and remember who you are.'

Both Rose and Sandy sat there and watched the corpulent man try and recover from his position. He looked up at them and smiled. 'Oops, I am not as young as I used to be, but can still chase you young things around the house. Don't you worry about that?'

They didn't react and Nic appreciated it. *The first test passed.*

Looking at Rose, then at Sandy, the Colonel laid on the charm. 'You two lovely ladies could do with a drink. Can I get something for you? Wow, this will be easy. One is a beautiful blonde, so obviously a sweet and light Chardonnay. For you, my pretty brunette, you must try the big bold red. It's delicious.'

Nic interjected. 'Sorry sir. Can I suggest they would just prefer sparkling water instead? They are due to meet with Commissioner Steldons at sixteen hundred.' And with that, the Colonel jumped back off the stage. 'Water it is then.'

The Colonel again miss-timed the step and bumped straight into Driver. Rose and Sandy did their best to stop laughing.

'Another fifteen minutes to go, so keep it together you two," Nic whispered. Rose leaned toward him. 'Fifteen-hundred? I thought this finished around three-thirty. We're famished Nic, when do we eat?'

'Ten minutes then.' Nic tapped at his watch, then nodded over to Driver, and another man. The two men took the prompt. Driver made his way up to the Colonel, where he was filling a plate from the table of finger food. Driver circled behind him, and the other man corralled the rest of the Colonel's entourage. All five of them.

One of the entourage came up to the Colonel. 'It's time to go, sir. I'm sorry you cannot stay any longer. It is nearing thirteen-thirty, and we have the meeting with Commission Steldons at fourteen hundred, sharp.' The Colonel looked at him, then gave a little wave to Rose and Sandy, blew them each a kiss, and called out. 'I'm sorry ladies can't stay for the show, business calls. Hope to see you a bit later though. I am so looking forward to it.' They ignored him.

The Colonel and his entourage left with Driver, and the other woman, whose name badge read 'Candy,' saw them to the escalators. When Driver returned to the room Nic let out a loud whistle. 'Pack it up boys', then he looked to Rose and Sandy. 'You two can relax now too. This show is now over.'

Rose and Sandy took a deep breath, stood up and headed towards the table of finger food, however as they arrived, the double doors behind the tables opened and a team of waiters and staff came through.

The waiting staff scooped the food from the tables, swept off the tablecloths, and made their way back out of the room. Another group had taken the wine bottles from the tables, loaded them onto trolleys, and left the room. The computer geeks had now started to move - the sound of snapping laptops went through the room, and everything was dropped into bags and boxes. It had the timing of a well-rehearsed orchestra.

Nic was watching everything. 'Ten minutes left, guys.'

The curtain shroud came down, the TV screens were folded into more boxes and everyone was rolling cables around their elbows. Two large black crates were rolled into the room and everything started going into them. Tables were folded up, the chairs stacked, and brooms were brought in.

Sandy noted the speed of everything. 'Wow, I think we should get these guys to clean our house, Rose.'

'Maybe, but who wants a house full of geeks?'

Someone called out; 'Done,' and another called out: 'Beer-o-clock. You beauty.'

Sandy looked at Nic. 'Hey Nick-o-las, when do we eat then? You took all the food away.' Rose grinned. 'You changed the appointment time with Commissioner Gordon. It's all part of the plan.'

Nic smiled. 'Yep, to that too, but it is Commissioner Steldons. Please don't call him Gordon, and I'm not Batman. Please remember that.'

They both saluted and Sandy added. 'Yes, Mr. Wayne. Oops sorry Mr. Thyme. Oops sorry I mean, Nick-o-las.'

Driver came up to them. 'Hey Nic, the boys did a good job. We still have about an hour to kill before we head up to meet the boss man.'

'What Nic, you have people in Adelaide that you want to kill too?' Rose asked with a wry smile. Nic responded quickly. 'Well, I can think of a least two, if you guys don't take me to Jetty Road for the best Chai Latte in Glenelg. Otherwise, you won't make it back to your Hotel tonight. Remember I have seen that secret room of yours, Rose.'

They looked at him and Sandy shook her head. 'Hey, you didn't even tell us about the other room. We found it by accident. What if we hadn't? We would've been slumming it in the single beds. You fink.'

Nic nodded. 'Hey, that's not fair. I would have told you......eventually. I *fink* I would've anyway.'

The four of them walked down Jetty Road, ordered coffees, Nic's chai latte, and an hour later were back in the car heading up to meet with the Commissioner in the CBD. Driver dropped them off at the Police HQ in Angas Street and he muttered something about not knowing how to handle a situation when the Police are nice to you. Nic grinned and the others laughed.

A sergeant let them into the building, ushered them to the waiting area, and at 16:00 Commissioner Steldons came out to meet them. He led them along the corridors and they passed his office. The door was closed and Rose noticed. 'It's no wonder it's closed, otherwise we might've seen the Bat phone. Is it red Nick-o-las?' Nic turned around. 'Not in here, I am Nic Thorn. You're Rose Palmer and Sandy Fraser.'

Sandy nodded. 'That's good. I mean if we were someone else and got picked up for illegally jaywalking across King William Street, we could just drop the Commissioner's name, and it would all be hunky-dory.'

The Commissioner overheard, stopped, turned around and they almost ran into each other. He looked at them. 'Have you met me before? I mean I might not even be Commissioner Steldons. I could be the real Batman doing a day job couldn't I?'

They were led along a corridor, entered a room of gathered Detectives and the group stood when the

Commissioner came in. He moved to the front and introduced Nic Thorn, Sandy Fraser and Rosemary Palmer to his team. A few of the officers came up and shook their hands. Nic took over when the Commissioner sat down. Rose noticed there was a whiteboard at the corner of the room that displayed two low-grade pixel photographs of whom she assumed were the scammers.

Nic started up. 'Thank you for your time today and for allowing me to run with this. Please be assured I am not part of the Police. I am a private citizen and my team understands we cannot operate outside the law. We are here to work with you for the duration of these operations. My Team has been working in Melbourne in conjunction with the Victorian Police, along with the Australian Federal Police. We are closing in on the unknown suspects.'

Nic took another moment before raising the connection to Adelaide. 'We believe they will be making an appearance at the Motor Show here this weekend, and whilst my team has sourced out the IP address, we need to catch them during the sting. Earlier this afternoon, we met with US Army's Lieutenant Colonel Franklin Georgette and he confirmed we are in a position to continue with the proposal. Any questions?'

'Excuse me, Mr Thorn, I'm Detective Kate Jenkins, the new lead on the investigation. I apologise for not being fully briefed, but how and why is the US Army making the fifteen Hummers available to be sold here in Australia? I mean the import duties and conversion to Right Hand Drive would surely prohibit the benefit to the end user?'

'Good question Detective Jenkins and thank you - the Hummers are not available at all. We approached the US Colonel to broker a deal for the Motor Trade Association of SA, VIC Roads and NSW Department of Transport. So, together with the Hummer Association of Australia, we are offering to supply and import them.' Nic paused for effect. 'We are implying the existence of the opportunity; it is nothing more than that. It is all about the play, the pre-sales and the invoice manipulation. At this stage, we believe the scammers have exceeded more than a million dollars, and that's all we know about. This is a cost to the Insurance Industry, the Motor Trade, and ultimately the integrity of the Australian way of life.'

The Commissioner stood and moved back to the front of the room. 'Ladies and gentlemen we will finish here, and Mr Thorn's Team will be back in touch with Detective Jenkins before Friday in readiness for the weekend.'

The room cleared, and a few of the officers again congratulated him on the progress of the investigation. The three of them were now alone in the room.

Sandy looked at Nic. "How do we get out of here Nic? I mean I didn't leave any bread crumbs, I was too hungry, and crikey, when you commented on the Australian way of life, I thought you were going to rip open your shirt, drop your dacks, and reveal to us that you were Superman, not Batman.'

Nic grinned. 'Well, let's go home Lois Lane, and you too Lexie Luther. I know the way out. I've been in this 'Bat cave' before.'

Driver was waiting outside and dropped them back at the Hotel. Sandy looked at Nic, smiled and batted her eyelashes. 'What's up for tomorrow then Nick-o-las? Can I please be Sandra Dee tomorrow? I mean this was fun.'

'Thanks, Sandy. Well, tomorrow is a free day and Driver will take you around, down to West Lakes Shopping Centre, Harbour Town, up to Burnside, and anywhere else you would like to go shopping.'

Driver looked at him horrified. 'I'll do what now?'

'Just kidding mate, they have my Business Credit Cards and can take a taxi instead - take the night off to spend with your boy, and at this stage, you won't be needed tomorrow either.'

Sandy grinned. 'Oh, wow, what's your boy's name? And can we meet him?'

'No, and no, Sandy.'

Sandy nodded. 'The boy's name is "No", and no, we can't meet him?'

Driver rolled his eyes as Rose and Sandy walked away. 'Nic, I can still find the time to drop them both off at the airport tonight if you need me to.'

Nic shrugged, then Driver drove away, and the three of them went into the Hotel foyer. 'Guys let's try the

'Shiki' It's here in the Hotel and is the best Japanese Restaurant in Adelaide. They do sushi and sashimi, plus teppanyaki dishes cooked at an open station.'

Rose nodded. 'So, it's not just a Sushi Train? But do they serve Soba? You know, the cold noodle dishes? Living alone, we'd assume you'd often have cold noodles for dinner, followed by cold pizza for breakfast, all served with cold beer.'

Nic shook his head. 'Yep, something like that. Please meet me there at seven and I'll show you a night to remember - eating-wise.'

It was 7 pm when Rose and Sandy entered the restaurant and saw Nic sitting inside at the bar dressed in a light blue suit with a bright red Patent leather tie, and matching bright red Patent leather loafers.

'Isn't he ever late, Sandy?'

The waitress bowed and welcomed them with 'Irrashaismasei,' Nic overheard, looked at Sandy and shook his head - was mouthing the word 'No', as they went up to him. 'I know what you were going to say, Sandy 'Hi, Rashi' or something like that, it's the oldest joke in the book of 'gaijin' humour.'

'Let me guess Nic, you speak Japanese?'

'Chisai - that means a little - but in your case, I could use 'koneko' which means 'small, like a baby cat.'

Sandy responded. 'Domo, Nick-o-las-san then.'

Nic nodded. 'Impressive.' Then Nic held up three fingers and asked the barman for Asahi beers.

Sandy grinned. 'Ah, 'beeru o'kudasai,' and that's about the extent of my Japanese.'

They took their drinks and the waitress showed them to their table, joining another group surrounding one of the teppanyaki stations. Nic whispered 'Remember you still have to be in character.' Both Rose and Sandy immediately sat to attention and bowed slowly in unison. Japanese style. The dinner and chef's presentation was impressive, and Rose mentioned a couple of times that it beats the Sushi Train hands down.

As they were nearing the end of the meal, Nic leant over and told them that he wanted to run over a few things with them, so they moved to a more private table. 'OK, I have about four things to run through.' They again slowly and politely bowed their heads. 'We're all ears, Nick-o-las.'

'Right, thanks I guess. Firstly.... Dog.'

Sandy looked at him horrified. 'That's disgusting Nic, this place is a reputable restaurant.'

Nic shook his head. 'No, I meant Dog at home, West End you know, the big fluffy thing. Who's looking after him?'

Rose nodded. 'Dave, our neighbour. We do have a cat flap, but Dog spends as much time as he can at his place too. Dog likes to eat whenever, wherever and whatever he wants, nothing gets between Dog and his kitty Dins.'

'Does he kill and eat the local wildlife then?'

Sandy smiled. 'Only the real slow and dumb ones. I mean, have you heard him running on our timber floorboards? It sounds like a herd of elephants.'

Nic smiled, then added. 'OK. Secondly, your thirtieth Birthday party Sandy.'

They looked at him. 'A bit presumptuous, Nic. Why did you even think you were going to get invited, and besides how do you know when it is?'

Nic looked at them, and Rose responded. 'Oh that's right, you know stuff and find out stuff, well sometimes you can get stuffed too.'

'No, that is not what I meant - it's the timing of it. I have wind of something that may involve some overseas travel, and might need one, or both of you to set things up with me.'

Rose shook her head. 'Tasmania or Phillip Island is not overseas Nic, so don't excite us like that. Besides, I have already been to Tasmania and found it soggy and wet.'

Nic grinned. 'That sounds like someone I picked up in the back of my taxi in Brisbane once.' Rose shook her head. 'Not funny, Nic.'

Nic continued: 'No, overseas, as in New Zealand or it could be Fiji. I just wanted to make you aware that both of those countries are outside of Australia.'

Rose sighed. 'Fiji sounds nice. Thirdly then, Nic?'

'Next week, if this goes down as it is supposed to on the weekend, it will be all over by Monday. So, on Tuesday, I am planning to head up to Pinnaroo to check out the re-cycling thing.'

Sandy shook her head. 'Count me out then. I'd like to go back on Monday morning. Carly rang and told me 'The Sweetened Plums' have a gig on Monday night. I'd like to be there.'

'Yup, you are good to go whenever you want, Sandy.'

Rose sighed again. 'So, what's number four?'

'Driver, at the Motor Show. He will be around, but you will not be able to use him or see him, he will make himself invisible."

Sandy nodded. 'Wow, he can actually do that. I didn't even know being invisible was a superpower anyway. I mean Wonder Woman uses an invisible jet, and I wonder how she finds it at the airport if it has been moved. Does she wander around aimlessly until she bumps into it?'

'No Sandy, she keeps the remote for the doors hidden in the golden wrist bracelets, and the head-lights beep on when she presses it. Honestly, I give up with you two and am going to bed. So, it's good night from me.'

Rose responded quickly. 'And goodnight from him.'

They watched him leave the restaurant and Sandy stood up. "You know, I still don't get what you two guys are on about with the goodnight thing.'

'It's from the two Ronnies, Sandy.'

'Who are they? Ronnie McDonald and Ronnie Woods?'

'No, we just watched the clown in the bright red Patent shoes leave us. It's Ronnie Corbett and Ronnie Barker, the English comedians from the mid-70s.' Rose then added. 'I get the Ronald McDonald reference, but who is Ronnie Woods?'

'He's from The Rolling Stones.'

'Oh, The Strolling Bones, and with that, I think it's time for me to stroll to bed.'

They started to make their way out of the restaurant, but just as they left the maître de hurried up to them. 'I am sorry ladies, but you haven't settled the bill.'

Rose grinned. 'Damn you Nick-o-las. You stiffed us with the bill.'

Sandy smiled and handed over the Business Credit Card. 'Here please put it on my card, oh, and add a fifty-dollar tip.'

CHAPTER 15

By late afternoon Thursday, they still hadn't heard from Nic. Sandy stood up and moved to the window. 'Have you got his number yet, Rose?'

'Nope.'

'Me neither, so let's walk across the road and see if he is in, and whether he would like to dine with us tonight.'

They walked across the road to the Stamford Plaza, went to reception, and asked to call his room. The receptionist made the call and hung up. 'Mr Thyme is in Room 23 on the second floor, however, has told me he needs about fifteen minutes. He has requested you please wait at the bar.'

They made their way over there, ordered a couple of glasses of Riesling, and after waiting the designated time both looked at their phones. He was late, and they were getting concerned.

They decided to see if they could at least get to his room. Fortunately, Rose overheard housekeeping was going to the second floor so they entered the lift Rose pretended to flash a card at the elevator button, but the maid had already waived her hand over the panel. They exited upon arriving on the second floor, heard a door shut somewhere in the hall, and a young woman hurried past them keeping her head down. She quickly moved toward the Emergency Exit stairs, opened the door and scampered away.

Rose and Sandy reached Room 23 and knocked on the door. Nic opened it. He was half-dressed and towel-drying his hair. 'I asked you to wait downstairs.' Nic promptly shut the door on them and they stood there.

Rose sighed. 'OK, well I guess that means we won't be having dinner with him tonight.'

They turned and went back to the elevator, returned to their Hotel and ordered room service. Sandy was sipping a Chardonnay. 'So what was that all about, and who was the woman that passed us? I mean do you think that she was visiting Nic?'

'Sandy, if she was, it is none of our business - I mean we don't own him.'

'Yeah but...'

'But nothing, Sandy. Let's put it behind us, and focus on what we have to do tomorrow. Let's have an early night and hopefully, I can get some sleep.'

'Nightcap not on then?'

'Nope, but thanks for the offer.' Rose went off to her room, flopped down on the bed and said aloud. 'All men are bastards.'

Sandy heard her, so replied through the wall. 'That they are, Rose.'

It was Friday morning, and Rose still didn't feel like breakfast but had to have something to settle her nerves. 'Hey Sandy, you go to breakfast and I'll come down a bit later'

A bit later had turned into forty-five minutes, and there was a knock at the door. It was Nic. 'Hey, c'mon down for breakfast. Sandy's down there waiting. She was worried, so sent me up here to collect you.'

Rose opened the door. 'How did you get up here - you need a card for the elevator and surely you haven't got the resources to override access to a security system operated by a multi-national hotel group? I mean, I think you are good at what you do, besides, I think I'm coming down with something.'

'Whoa, both of you are a bit snippy this morning. I mean, what's up?' Nic held out a room pass. 'I used Sandy's card.'

Rose sighed. 'Surely you have some idea, Nick-o-las?'

'Oh, the thing last night outside my room? I need to trust that you both have my six o'clock. I did ask that you wait in the bar.'

Rose sighed again. 'Let me tidy myself up, and I'll join you down there in fifteen.'

'It's a date.'

'No, it's not, Nic. It's a job.'

Nic turned and left, and Rose waited to hear the elevator chime before shutting the door, then grabbed her handbag, shook herself a few times and stared into the mirror. *'Rose, it was never going anywhere. You should expect your men to be short fat and shallow. You know that the TD&H's pass you by without a second look.'*

Rose was all business when she met them in the breakfast parlour. Nic went over the details of the plan. 'It's all about the invoice manipulation guys, rather than the show we must put on. Everything else is the diversion. The goal is the trap, not the glue holding it all together. I assume you guys have heard of it. PDF writer? Well, we're going to make it so simple that they can't pass up the opportunity.'

Rose nodded. 'PDF Writer' means they have computer software that can over-write un-editable documents. So what's the trick?'

Nic nodded. 'Our invoices are in WORD.doc.'

Sandy leaned forward. 'That's stupid Nic. Surely, it's not coming down to that?'

'Yep, we want them to come in all guns blazing. Whilst they're putting it all through as quickly as they can, we'll be watching the Internet Protocol traffic to see where it's being originated from. We're not expecting the scammers to be over-sophisticated, just greedy.'

Sandy added. 'So, do you have any real buyers

ready to commit to the transfer of funds during the show, or is everything done afterwards?'

'Good question. We know that five of the Hummers have already been 'ordered', and are to be paid in full during the weekend show. These are to be spread over Friday, Saturday and Sunday. Any questions from you Rose?'

'No, and it is Rosie. Remember, Nick-o-las?'

'Yep, and from now on, everybody will be watching us, everything is on show, and everything matters.' Rose nodded again. 'Got it loud and clear, Nick-o-las.'

Nic tapped his phone. 'So, we all meet out the front of the Convention Centre, at eleven. It's nine-thirty now, so go back and get ready. You won't miss me. I'll be standing next to a dirty great big ex-US Army Hummer, and most likely the Colonel will be there too.'

'It's a date, Nic-o-las.'

'No, Rosie it's a job, and this is not a rehearsal. No time for mistakes, and if you want to walk away now you can. I won't mind, and Rose, there is no safety word this time. It could get really ugly, and we don't know who we are dealing with.'

At 11.00 am, Rose and Sandy left the hotel and crossed the promenade to the Convention Centre. Nic saw them coming and could only just keep himself from smiling as they both looked amazing. They were both beautifully turned out. The Colonel noticed too, and Nic slapped his hand down from his mouth. 'Not appropriate, Colonel.'

'Mr Thyme. Don't ever touch me again, son.'

Rose had overheard the comment and smiled. There was now quite a gathering around the Hummer, and the Colonel was in his element.

Meantime, Rose and Sandy just stood there and watched Commissioner Steldons arrive. He directly approached Nic and asked where Rosie and Sandra were. Nic nodded over to them.

'Good show, Mr Thyme.'

More patrons were collecting around the entrance, so Nic moved around to Rose and Sandy 'Time to move inside, please, ladies.' He politely led them into the foyer where a table showing the names of the VIP guests and partners was set up. Rose called over to Nic, directing him to the table. 'Please locate our name tags Nick-o-las.' The Colonel was standing nearby. 'I bet she's a ball-breaker that one.' Nic smiled, thinking *'Yep good job, Panda-Eyes,'*

Nic offered to pin the badges on. They both declined. 'Lanyards only, please, Nick-o-las. Remember who we are.' They bowed their heads which allowed him to carefully place the lanyards over their necks.

The group stepped inside the auditorium. It was immense, full of beautiful cars and beautiful women standing next to them. Nic reminded them their stall was on the right-hand side, and they should now make their way there. This time they led him, and the Colonel managed to let out a wolf whistle. '*What? What?* They overheard him saying. '*So many beautiful things in here. A Bird Colonel can whistle if wants to can't he?*'

They arrived at the stall, and everything was set up the same as they had seen at The Grand Hotel. Candy was in full performance mode with her PowerPoint presentation, however, about fifteen men were watching her this time. Rose raised her head toward the gathered group.

'I see Candy is back again, Nick-o-las. I thought that we'd specifically requested that we were not outshone by anyone else.'

Nic looked over. 'Candy? Who is that? Oh you mean her. She is not one of mine. She came with the Colonel's entourage.'

Rose whispered. 'If she is with him Nic, would you mind keeping an eye on the Colonel then? I mean, we saw what you did to Michael for me. Maybe you offer some guidance to the Colonel?'

'Duly noted Rose, but I might leave it a day or two. I'll have a word to Driver and get him to look after her.'

Rose grinned. 'So, we might see the invisible man around here after all?'

'Not likely.' Nic then showed them to a small space behind the curtain. 'This is a private space to use when you need to have a rest. Remember you still have the roles to play, so be vigilant and report any suspicious activities. Take a break as often as you like, but don't overdo it, as I need both of you out here too.'

Sandy nodded. 'When and where do we eat then, Nic?'

'In here, but only one of you at a time, sorry. Candy will be using it too, so you may get to know her, but remember to remain in character. She might be a part of the problem, not the cure.'

Rose nodded. 'I'll take the first shift Sandy, and be back in about an hour. I'll see if I can find a nice new husband or at least a nice new car. The odds are in my favour I'll find the car first.'

Nic stood next to Sandy and tried to explain about the woman in his Hotel Room to clear the air, but she turned away. 'It's none of my business Nick-o-las, who or what you do in your spare time. It is not in my care either, so please do not speak of it again.' Sandy then moved towards Candy, still within the confines of their stall.

One of the geeks overheard the comment and came up to him. 'Wow, what was that all about? Is she for real? I mean who is she anyway?'

Nic bowed his head. 'I work for them, and they expect impeccable behaviour from me at all times.' Nic then heard a muffled laugh from behind the curtain, he turned and parted the black folds. Driver was standing amongst the fabric.

'I see Panda-Eyes got the first shift Nic, so good luck with that, and yes, I'll look out for Candy too. I've done some snooping on our Colonel Georgette. He has quite a reputation with the ladies. I assume that's why he's looking after Supply here in Australia rather than the real Army work in the US. I reckon he's got one more allegation against him, so give me the word and it will be fried chicken for the Colonel in Fort Leavenworth.'

Nic grinned. 'Thanks, mate, and be careful as it looks like Panda-Eyes is coming back over here to see why I am talking to the curtain.'

CHAPTER 16

It was nearing 16:00, and they had sent a few WORD.doc invoices, but emails had only come back with suggestions the document should be in. PDF. *"We would appreciate that re-send your invoice in .pdf before we proceed with our purchase."* Nic was happy with that.

Rose and Sandy had seen as much as they wanted and wanted to call it a day, so Nic agreed. 'We still have Saturday and Sunday to go, and we are all due to meet with Detective Jenkins for a debrief at eighteen hundred.' He watched them go, and Driver stepped out from behind the curtain again. 'Anything to report Nic? I won't be joining the chat with the Police either if that's OK.'

'Sure, mate. Me, nothing to report. How about you?'

'Just a feeling. Something is going on with Candy and the Colonel. I don't know what it is quite yet, but just have a feeling. I also think that one of those Army guys, and Candy are hooked up somehow too. Again, nothing but a hunch.'

Nic nodded. 'OK, well finish up now, and please

take your boy on that ropey thing down by the West Beach caravan park. I reckon you have a couple of hours of daylight left.'

'Thanks, mate, and see you in the morning. Oh, and am I still right to go back home to Victor Harbor on Monday morning with my boy?'

"Yep, hopefully, this gets all shut down tomorrow, so we can have Sunday off."

18:00, and the meeting was in one of the rooms in the basement of Parliament House. Nic was already there when Sandy and Rose arrived. The Colonel was there too, along with a couple of the Army personnel. They were all collected around the data printouts. Candy's absence, along with one of the other Army staff was conspicuous, at least to Nic, so he broached their absence with the Colonel, but it was dismissed as not being relevant.

The Colonel started up. 'Why has my dinner been interrupted son, and why is this Detective Jenkins explaining to me that the whole Hummer proposal was a ruse? Simply the bait to flush out some invoice scammers? I demand to know who had the authorisation to waste my time on such trivial matters as the integrity of the Australian Motor Trade.'

Commissioner Steldons walked in, and Rose whispered to Sandy. 'Wow, I didn't even see the bat signal in the sky. He's turned up anyway.'

'Now, what were you saying, Colonel? Do you have

an issue with Nic and his Team regarding the invoicing integrity and safety of the payments? If you do, you can discuss it with me, or the other Police Units here in Australia. We need your assistance to continue with the event tomorrow and are seeking your ongoing commitment. Remember you and your entourage are guests in our country.'

Nic nodded his appreciation to the Commissioner.

It was nearing 19:00. Sandy and Rose told Nic they were leaving, and he leaned forward to respond. 'Let's meet again out the front of the venue next to the Hummer tomorrow. It was all still going ahead as planned, so I will skip dinner with you two, and see you in the morning.'

Rose and Sandy were led away and stepped into the warm evening air. 'Hey, Rose. Have you managed to see Driver in the Motor Show as yet?'

'No, but did you notice how often Nic stands with his back to the curtain and talks to himself?'

'Yes, I saw that. Did you get a chance to talk to Candy as yet?'

'Sorry, I forgot to tell you. Candy and one of the other Army guys have a thing going. It's early stages, but she says it's serious, and the Colonel is not happy about it at all. That is probably why she's not here tonight. They were going to see the sights of Adelaide, then have an early night.'

'It's only just after seven, Sandy.'

'I know right, maybe there are not many sights to see, but we had better tell Nic about Candy and the Army dude anyway. It may mean nothing, but it may mean everything. Didn't they teach you that in the school of Nancy Drew?'

'No. as I could never get over Parker Stephenson and Shaun Cassidy as the Hardy's boys.'

'That was the late 70's...'

'Yes, it was.'

'You weren't even born.'

'I love watching re-runs on Netflix, along with their tight pants and fluffy hair.'

'You're terrible Rose-Muriel.'

Making their way outside and back towards the Hotel, they noticed a man in his mid-20s and a woman in her early 50s over by the Hummer. They were walking around it, patting the door panels, checking the locks and windows, and were taking an extra-ordinary time about it. The man was now busying himself trying to work out the locking mechanism on the bonnet.

Rose whispered to Sandy 'Can you take a picture but reverse the camera to take a photo the other way.'

Sandy nodded. 'Sure, but why?'

Rose added louder this time. 'Can you please take a selfie of us, Sandra? These Hummers are such beautiful machines.'

Sandy whispered. 'Sure, but how do we play this? Tourists? Swedish Students? Two ladies out on the town?'

Rose whispered in response. 'Nope, just remain in character. We're two lovely ladies wanting a picture in front of a lovely Hummer.'

'That's disappointing.'

They got closer, made some poses and Sandy took the picture. It took longer than they wanted as they were trying to get both of the loiterers in the one snap, but eventually decided one of each would work just as fine. The loitering couple must have suspected something as they suddenly moved away by going down the cement ramp towards North Terrace.

'Do you want to follow them?'

'Sure, but make sure we keep our distance. We don't want to overplay it.'

Rose and Sandy waited, then made their way to the street level to catch a glimpse of the mysterious couple. When they stepped from the protection of the building, and onto the footpath, they noticed that the couple was gone.

Suddenly, a late model white Commodore was bearing towards them, and they had to jump out of the way. It mounted the footpath and then careened up the road. Sandy took a breath. 'That was close. Were they the same couple?'

'I've no idea, and that was a bit too risky, we could've been killed.'

Sandy nodded. 'There was that, but given we're dressed in these pretty party outfits we would have made nice-looking corpses. I did manage to take photos of the car - both the front and back.'

'OK, we'll let Nic know. It's now seven-thirty, let's walk over to Hindley Street to get a nightcap, but it may be too early to flash around the Business Credit Card, so we'd better use cash.'

Rose then noticed Nic crossing the road up a little from them. He was arm-in-arm with a woman and smiling - she could've been the same one that rushed passed them in the hallway, but they didn't know. Nic didn't see Rose and Sandy as they were hidden by the scaffolding surrounding the building.

'Hey, can we go to the Railway Station instead? I have heard there is a new pub there. I've just lost my appetite, and the clubbing confidence, sorry.'

Sandy noticed Rose was still staring towards the space where Nic and the young woman had been, despite them having already moved into the Stanford Hotel. 'That's fine, but just so you know, it is a four-hour drive to Pinnaroo, and unless you shake whatever funk you are in every time you see Nic with another woman, it's going to be a very quiet and lonely drive.'

Rose shrugged. 'Well, there is that.'

CHAPTER 17

It was nearing 16:00 again, and Saturday was un-eventful. Rose had managed to chat with the buyer of the Mercedes 300SL. He had shipped it down from Brisbane for the event. Rose wondered why Nic hadn't mentioned that the car was the main attraction.

Meantime, Sandy was spending more time with Candy, and still trying to find Driver. It was a quiet moment, so she sat down with Nic.

'Hey Nic, can I get another name please?'

'What's wrong with Sandy Olsson?' Sandy sighed. 'Well, Rose is Miss Panda-Eyes, and Candy is Miss Eye-Candy. So, can you come up with something special for me?'

Nic wondered where the conversation was going, but played along anyway. 'Sure, I have a couple. Andy Pandy: Handy Andy and one of my favourites is Sandy Brandy, who looks quite dandy.'

'You're just rhyming my name with itself, Nic. Can't you come up with something better?'

Nic sat down. 'No, and why would I want to? You are Sandy, and you are terrific and beautiful and funny and everything that...well I....' Nic suddenly stopped talking, stood up and Sandy looked up. 'Whoa, what are you saying?'

Nic looked at her, and Sandy continued. 'I mean, I thought you and Rose had something, but then you dumped her and moved onto "Miss Run Quickly Past Us" in the Hotel Corridor, "Miss Arm in Arm whilst You Cross the Street". Has she dumped you and you're hitting on me now?'

Nic took a breath. 'What are you talking about?'

'The day you told us off in the Hotel. Rose had said something about having your six, we don't even know what that means.'

Nic was now a little confused. 'It means whilst I am watching forward, you are watching my back. Twelve is out front, six is behind, three to the left and nine to the right. It's Army talk, that sort of stuff, but who's this woman you are talking about? Oh, how many times have you seen us? I thought we were being discreet.'

Sandy sighed. 'Well, twice, and will we get to meet her?'

'No, I said I didn't want you to meet her.'

'I don't think so. We'd remember if you had mentioned someone hanging around the forbidden tree of Mr Nic Thorn.'

'She's my sister. Damn it.'

Sandy looked around. 'Where?'

'Well, as of right now in my Hotel room at the

Stamford Plaza, but please don't tell Rose. So this is what is it all about? The snippy comments, and the long faces. Oh crap. I have to get her out of there. If you've seen her twice, that's bad. It's bad for my business, bad for me, and bad for her.'

Sandy wondered what was going on, and Nic continued: 'And Sandy, I almost have lost my two new best friends over it too.'

Sandy was now confused. 'C'mon Nic. What two new best friends? And how did you lose them? Where did they go?'

'You and Rose. I mean I count Driver as a friend too, but he works for me.'

'We're working for you at the moment too, aren't we?'

'True, but when this job is over I'll pay Driver and he'll disappear for a while until I need him again. I pay him well, and that's why he keeps finding the time to work for me. Besides he lives here in South Australia. With you guys it's different. I mean, I hope that when this is over and we all go back to Brisbane, we keep whatever we have going. It's only been a month or something. You guys make everything I do seem worthwhile and a little less dark. Sometimes it gets very lonely doing what I do.'

'Whoa, Nic. That was a lot to know, I mean, you and me and Rose. We could be like the Three Musketeers of Oz?'

'There's more to it Sandy. Everything has an angle

and a back story, and my job requires me to spend a lot of time on my own. So, you guys are annoyed at me because I let my guard down, and spent some time with my sister? I can't let you meet her though. It could get dangerous dealing with some of the people that I deal with, like Colonel Creepy over there.'

'How do you keep altogether? Doesn't it wear you down?'

Nic sighed. 'Well, it does sometimes, but don't dare tell anyone what I just said, otherwise, I might have to kill you.'

'You told us that you don't kill people.'

'Yes, I did, but I also said I *could* make an exception.'

Sandy got up and looked at him. She started to walk away, then ran back to him and breaking out of character, hugged him before taking off again.

Meanwhile, Driver had been standing in the folds of the curtains, drew them back, walked up to Nic and hugged him too. They pulled back, looked at each other, held out their hands, and firmly shook them instead.

'I'll go to the Hotel and get her Nic, and organise someone to get her home ASAP. You are right though, in your line of work you can't afford to make mistakes, and by the way, great speech. I heard most of it, and that is why you're the best at what you do. You say the word mate, and I'll relocate to Brisbane if you need me up there, but by the sounds of it, you will have your hands full with those two. They are a blast, and unlike most people, I never tire of being around them. Keep them close, Nic. When you find people like them, don't let them go.'

'Thanks, mate, and for everything you do, not just as a...well, you know.'

Rose came up just as Driver folded himself back into the curtains, she saw movement behind Nic, so dodged around him and pulled the curtain back. There was nothing there.

'Hey, Nick-o-las. Did you say something to Sandra? She was in a hurry when she went past me. I was going to show her the latest McLaren.'

'I think you'll have to ask her that.'

'Secrets. So many secrets Nic. I may be jaded, but at least I don't keep secrets.'

'This whole thing we are doing in here is one giant secret - you do keep them.'

'This is different, this is the job, and there are commitments to your employer, so they are not true secrets anyway. However, I found out something interesting. Douglas told me how much you sold the Mercedes to him for, and then he showed me how much you bought it for. It's no wonder you have a place in Brisbane and one in Adelaide. You made a good profit on the flip. It was almost the same profit for you in one transaction, as we did in the seven years we had 'The She Shed.'

'Yep. That's part of what I do, match supply and demand. I buy stuff, sell stuff, find stuff and lose stuff, and a lot of people keep telling me I am doing a good job. I hope you and Sandy will be one of those people too, Rose.'

Rose was about to respond when Candy and a young man came bounding up to them. 'We have found something Nick-o-las. For two days Delray has been going through all the I.T. traffic. I mean he came to my room last night and well, ignored me for five hours while working on it. He's found something. He's saying it's an anomaly, but he's found a pattern.'

'But you two guys don't work for me, Candy.'

The young cadet walked over. 'Yes, Mr Thyme, isn't it? We do not. My name is Private First Class Delray DeMille, sir. I think I've found what you've been looking for.'

Nic went all business and asked them what they were talking about. Delray started spouting about what he had found. Nic listened a little then held his hand up indicating to stop talking, and called over to his geek people. 'Jonty, Fergal, Callum. Can you come over here, please? I need you to hear something.'

Jonty stood up. 'Sure Nic, sorry Nick-o-las, oops Mr Thyme.'

Nic then asked Candy and Rose to step outside, and he drew the curtains so no one could come in. Rose stepped forward. 'Thank you for the direction, Nick-o-las, but what will we tell anyone who *wants* to come and look?'

Nic smiled. 'Please tell them we are having a sales de-briefing, and the exhibit is closed for the day.'

Rose nodded. 'Thank you. But sorry one last question, Mr. Thyme. What if someone wants to buy a Hummer?'

'I am sure you will think of something, Miss Rhynge.'

Rose and Candy stepped out of the exhibit, pulled the black curtains over the entrance and took a position on either side. They could only just make out the conversation going on behind them. Rose was hoping that no one would come up to them as she had no idea how to sell a Hummer, or even to take details for an order.

They stood there and waited for a couple of minutes, then Candy looked over at Rose. 'You know Delray is very smart. He's managing to study at M.I.T. while we are here in Adelaide. This thing here is all part of his plans, but I am happy to see where the road takes me. You know, I don't want to get to your age and not have seen much of this beautiful world before Global Warming takes it all away. Just how old are you Miss Rhynge, nearly forty?'

'Not exactly Candy.'

'Well, he knew things were not right when he saw you Wednesday at The Grand Hotel thing. He'd seen you somewhere before, but couldn't work it out as you looked different somehow. Then someone mentioned Brisbane, and it clicked with him so he showed me the clip from the net. Just what are you doing here in Adelaide, Miss Panda-Eyes?'

Rose didn't know where to look or what to say and was about to respond, but then saw Douglas the 300SL Mercedes owner, making a bee-line for her. He was smiling, and Rose started to panic.

'Hello, Miss Rhynge. My friend here Elliott and I were just leaving and passed that impressive beast of yours outside. I mentioned to him that I knew you were working with the group that was selling the Hummers, and guess what? We have decided to buy one each. It will go beautifully parked in my garage next to the Mercedes 300SL, and who knows I may even drive the Hummer to the shops instead of my Maybach Rolls Royce.'

Candy noticed the look of panic on Rose's face, smiled at them, and stepped forward. 'If I may gentlemen. Thank you for taking the opportunity to purchase the vehicles. I am more than happy to take the details from you right now. Are you looking to pay a deposit or the complete purchase price? If you do pay in full, I will waive my commission, and that would save you around two thousand dollars each.'

Rose again didn't know where to look or what to say, apart from thinking that Candy may have just saved the whole shebang. Candy then politely guided them to the nearest desk, sat them down, offered them a coffee each, and went through the whole sales process. Then started referencing the fluctuations in

AUD v US currencies, even offering to lock in the exchange rate with '*her people*'.

Rose realised she was a little out of her league, and when both gentlemen agreed to pay the full cost on the spot, suddenly had a thought. 'Would you like me to assist you with the preparation of the Invoices Miss....sorry Candy?'

Candy looked over to Rose and gave her a million-dollar smile, 'No, but thank you for the offer though Miss Panda-Eyes. I can complete it here all on my Tablet.'

Douglas heard that reference and must have wondered what it was about. Rose looked at him and held her breath, but he shrugged his shoulders, so she breathed out again. He patted Elliott on the arm. 'Where do we sign Candy? And Elliott, it looks like we have just bought matching Hummers. What a bargain.'

Candy continued: 'Can I please have your email addresses? I will send invoices to you and they will be re-submitted as 'fully paid' once we receive the full amount. Thank you for your patronage, and please enjoy the rest of your time at the Adelaide Motor Show.'

The two gentlemen provided their details, checked their phones, nodded that they had received the invoices, sent a confirmation email back, and then moved away.

'I did a good job didn't I Miss Panda-Eyes? I mean you had no idea what to do did you?'

'No, I didn't, and thank you. How did you know what we were doing here?'

'Delray did some snooping after he showed me the clip from GOMA, he wondered if there were other things in play too. He managed to link into some chatter between your little Hummer groups, then saw the name Nic, rather than Nick-o-las a few times, then another name Thorn, and did some research on the name Nic Thorn. He found some more chatter on invoice manipulation in some random SA Police chatroom and put two and two together. All of this on Thursday instead of taking me down to McLaren Vale for a winery tour, and by Friday night he had written some coding to filter out the traffic from the Wi-Fi here at the Convention Centre. And *that* is what he is explaining right now to your Nic Thorn and his cohorts behind this curtain.'

'Thanks again, Candy. I think you and Delray have just closed the loop.'

'Do you know much about Nic Thorn yourself? Rose Palmer isn't it, not Rosie Rhynge? That's quite nasty too. I assume it was his idea to call you Ringa-Rosie? And what's with Sandra Olsson too? I assume you know that Sandra Olsson is Sandy from Grease?'

'Yes. It's all Nic's idea not to use our real names.' Rose hesitated. 'What did you find about Nic though? I mean Sandy and I have only known him about a month.'

Candy smiled. 'Well, he was born in Ouyen, Victoria and has a twin sister that lives in Murrayville.'

Rose nodded. 'Yes we know that, but Nic will not let us meet her. It's something about the protection of family, and all the secrecy to do with his job.'

Candy nodded. 'I get that, but did you know that his sister is currently in Adelaide? I believe she's staying across the road at the Stamford Plaza.'

Rose looked at her.

Just then Nic stepped out through the curtain and beckoned them to come back inside. 'So, did you two have fun talking girly stuff whilst Delray filled us in on what he has done?'

Rose nodded. 'Well actually Nic, Candy managed to sell two Hummers, took the details, invoiced them, got two responses back, and also told me a little more about the man who is Nic Thorn.' She paused for his response.

'Sold them to who?'

'To Douglas, your Mercedes SL300 buyer, and his friend Elliott.'

Delray approached them. 'We already have a hit, Nic. The two invoices that went out just then have just bounced back with the account numbers changed.'

Rose then realised Nic had only responded to her comment about the sale of the Hummers, so stood there waiting for more from him, but nothing was offered.

Nic stepped back into the exhibition. 'Let's wrap it up guys, and we make the play first thing tomorrow. Candy and Delray, a big thank you.' Candy smiled and gave Delray a light peck on the cheek. 'Will do Nic, and see you in the morning,'

Nic collected a few things and started moving toward the exit.

'Are you coming Miss Rhynge?'

CHAPTER 18

The Motor Show was due to start at 13:00, so at around 10:30 Rose emerged from her room, but Sandy wasn't in hers, nor were her suitcases, so she called her number. *'I am sorry the number you have reached is currently unavailable.'*

Damn it, Sandy. Where are you?

Rose went to dial Nic's but realised he still had not given it to her, so she rushed downstairs, across the road to the Stamford Plaza, and pleaded with the desk to call Room 23. It didn't answer, so Rose convinced the clerk to issue her a visitor's pass for the elevator. Rose made her way up there and knocked on the door, and a woman opened it.

'I'm sorry I am looking for Nick-o-las Thyme. This is his room.'

'No one here by that name. We've just flown in from London. Have been asleep as they allowed us an early check-in.'

Rose resolved he wasn't there, so returned downstairs and handed the pass back. 'The man in Room 23, Nic Thyme. Did he check out?'

'Yes, last night. I'm sorry you didn't ask for him, only the Room Number.'

'So, is he still here then?'

'No, his Driver collected him last night. He didn't say where he was going. Can I take you're your number and have him call you if he comes back?'

'No, that's OK Sorry, I have one more question. Was there someone else registered in the room with him?'

The receptionist located the booking details. 'Here let me have a look. Yes, there was a woman, and in this case, Would you like to know her name?'

Rose held her breath. 'That would be good, thank you.'

'Here it is.... Oh no, sorry it only says '+1."

Rose muttered: 'Damn you Nic'

Rose gave up on the idea of tracking him down and trudged her way back to the Hotel. She missed the man sitting there reading the Sunday Mail in the red Patent leather shoes, but he didn't miss her.

'Why do you look so sad, Miss Panda-Eyes?'

She stopped and the man dropped his paper, stood up, they hugged, and she punched him in the shoulders. 'What's going on, Rose?'

'Sandy's gone.'

'Yep, I know. She flew back to Brisbane on a red-eye. She told me she didn't want to wake you and also told me to tell you something else.' Nic held two fingers up to symbolise a quotation: "*Now that you both know about my sister, can you drop it please?*"

Rose smiled. 'No way, not until we meet her. Will we ever get to meet her?'

'Nup, but you might get close. We'll be in Pinnaroo on Tuesday and she lives in Murrayville.'

'How close will that be?'

'About twenty-five kilometres. Oh, and by the way, wouldn't you like to change to a single room? You can't possibly share a huge two-bedroom suite all alone.'

'You could've come in with me, Nic. I mean king-size beds in each room. I'm sure we wouldn't have bumped into each other.'

'Yep, I entirely agree, but the door lock is on your room side only. How could I have possibly kept you from coming into my room? You might have laughed at my Winnie the Pooh pj's?'

'We could have swapped rooms.'

'I thought about that too, but that would have meant the onus was on me to keep out of your room, and you don't wear any pj's at all.'

'That's not true. Who told you that?'

'Your cat, Dog. He knows all your secrets.' Rose shrugged. 'Do I need to do anything with the luggage or clothes?'

'Nup, I can get that taken care of by the Hotel. I have moved in here now too; separate rooms, separate floors, separate everything.'

'So, what now then?'

'We start again at thirteen hundred. Let's have a

quick lunch, and then you can go off and do your magic with that fairy dust that keeps you looking beautiful. Let's then meet back at the Hummer stand.'

'OK, I forgot to mention Sandy took some pictures of the Hummer. A couple was hanging around it and they looked like they were trying to carjack it. We think they tried to run us down with their car, a Commodore, maybe? Could they steal the Hummer Nic?"

Nic pulled out his phone, scrolled through the photos and showed them to Rose. "This white one? Sandy sent them to me and funny about the car though. No registration plates on the front or the back, but there is no point in doing that as the Vehicle Identification Number by the driver's side is always visible. It's a near-new RS model that was purchased in June 2019 in Griffith NSW, paid sixty grand for it in cash, and it's registered to Mrs Marilyn, 'Mar' Ann Bakker of RSD 1105, Barren Box Swamp. That too is interesting, as Mar doesn't hold a license anymore. It was suspended two months ago for speeding on The Hamilton Highway, just east of Lismore."

'I've been through there. It's west of Geelong. Does that mean something?'

'Not in isolation, but this couple, driving a nearly new Commodore, paid for in cash. Who lives in a country town away from prying eyes, has a suspended licensed driver, and is in Adelaide whilst a Motor Show is on, who then tried to run you down just because you were taking their photograph. If I was suspicious at all, I would say probably. I'll get my guys to find out about them and tell you what, I'll run a competition between my guys and against your new BFF Candy, and her beau. I'll put up five-grand to whoever finds a link between the un-subs, and these guys if it turns out to them."

Rose grinned. 'Wow, a five-grand bonus, but what if it does turn out to be them? It was us, your super sleuths, Nancy Drew and Miss Marple that provided the crumb.' Nic nodded. 'Mm, OK. I might have to re-think what I am paying you.'

'You haven't paid us anything yet.'

Nic grinned. 'Yep, well there is that too - as for the Hummer out the front, they won't get far, as it doesn't even have an engine.'

It was 13:00. Rose drew back the black curtain at the exhibition and stepped in. This time she was dressed in a midnight blue sheath, split thigh high. The wedge sandals were complimented by a small clutch. Some of the geeks saw her enter and turned to look. The rest stopped what they were doing, and one had his pen drop out of his mouth onto the floor.

Nic saw the movements, or lack thereof, and turned to look. 'Nice'.

Candy approached her. 'Sorry about the nearly forty comment, Rose.'

'That's OK Candy. What is the latest around here?'

'Well, Nic has challenged my lone Delray against

the three of his guys. They are trying to find the link between these unsubs, and Mar Bakker from Griffith. They're saying there isn't one, but Del is not convinced. He is chasing down the IP, and they are going for the I.T. So much geek, it's all giving me the S.h.i.' Rose smiled at the attempted rhyme. 'Let's go for a walk then. Have you been in a Hummer before?'

'Nope, but we do have big trucks where I come from. We call them Julies.'

Rose looked at her. 'You use a girl's name to describe a big manly truck?'

Candy looked at her. 'No, dualies…as in a dual axle.'

Rose realised the connection and nodded. 'Well, I have the keys to the Hummer, but we can't drive it though."

'Because it is Left Hand Drive? I would be able to drive it, Rose.'

'Not really, as Nic mentioned something to do with missing a major component.'

They made their way towards the exit, and by the time they were close to the front door, they had an entourage. Candy looked behind her. 'All of these men looking at these beautiful cars, and they just want to follow us instead? What's that all about, Rose?'

'Just how old *are* you Candy?'

'I'm nineteen. Why, do you want to go for a drink later? I mean, it's too young in the States but here, Down Under it's only eighteen, you know.'

'Yes, I knew that. Just checking.'

Rose went around the Hummer, unlocked the door and looked in. There was nothing but a large empty shell. The driver's seat was on the left, the dashboard was partially complete and the steering column was in place.

Meantime, Candy was holding her hands up against the blackened windows, and some of their entourage were trying to have a look inside. 'I can't see anything inside. The windows are too black.'

Rose then heard a comment, as it came with a lurid connotation: '*Oh, I can see though.*' Rose stepped back from the Hummer and realised the comment had come from the Colonel, so she shut the door and re-locked it. He was standing closely behind Candy. Rose noticed that Nic was heading directly for the Colonel and took him by the arm, and wondered if he was breaking character to protect Candy or if something else was happening.

Nic nodded to Driver, who had just arrived in their car with a squeal of tyres. 'I am sorry Sir, we have an urgent request from Commissioner Steldons. You are to meet immediately at Police HQ, in Angas Street.'

They manhandled him into the rear seat, much to his protest. Nic then sat down beside him, and Rose glimpsed the light of an iPad. The door shut, the car stayed where it was for a couple of moments, then Nic stepped out and it drove away.

Candy walked over to them. 'Hey, where did the Colonel go? I mean did he go back to the Hotel, or did all my prayers come true, and he's finally on the way back to the US of A?'

Nic nodded. 'Almost Candy, but unfortunately I couldn't quite do that. I reminded him that he's a guest in our country, and should behave himself at all times. Especially around young ladies like yourself.'

Rose went back into character. 'So, what's up next, Nick-o-las?'

'Everything, Rosie. The bait, the honey and the bees. Delray won the comp with the IP trail. It led him back to a provider based in Griffith. "Growing our Future.com.au." So, let's get back in there.'

Candy and Rose followed him back inside and had to remind him to slow down a couple of times as they were both in high heels and tight dresses. The entourage that had followed them outside was now following them back in. Every time the ladies had to stop, the crowd cheered, but at the end of the parade, the crowd booed when they stepped inside the exhibit.

Nic shut the curtains behind them. 'Where are we up to guys?'

'Well Delray is still following the Service Provider, and we are monitoring the Wi-Fi in this auditorium.' Fingers were flying across keyboards. Callum sat back, put his hands behind his head and entwined his fingers. 'We've got him.'

'Where is the son-of-a-?' This comment came from Commissioner Steldons. Rose turned to Candy. 'Wow, he must be Batman. We didn't even see him come in here.'

'He is not Batman. It's not real Rosie, and super-heroes don't exist as all the Unicorns scared them away.' Rose nodded. 'That may be true Candy, but there are superheroes - they wear Army fatigues instead of capes. If Delray is the one for you Candy, hold him tight and don't let him go.'

'He's here.' This time it was Delray.

'Where? Surely not here in Adelaide? That would be too close. Too easy.'

'Not just in Adelaide, he's here in this building.'

Callum called out 'So how do we find him? He unlocked his fingers, cracked them, and had them poised over his keyboard ready to charge into battle once again. Nic called out. 'Send out another bogus invoice, but this time make it for four Hummers at two hundred and fifty grand. If I'm right he won't pass it up, and let's make it even easier. Leave the account number off the invoice altogether to see if he bites and chews on that.'

Callum set it up and they waited, and waited, but nothing happened.

After about an hour Candy announced she couldn't stand it anymore, and some of the geeks were bored and started to play online to battle with another League of Legends. Delray, however, still had his focus, and Nic noticed.

Rose approached Candy. 'Come on, let's go for a

walk, and have a last look at all these cars. Keep a look out for anything suspicious though, anything that doesn't fit.'

They stepped outside the exhibit and began to walk around. 'How long have been doing this investigation stuff with Nic?'

'About a month?'

'Wow, what were you before? Police, Armed Services, Private Investigators? Delray couldn't find anything on you at all, but there was a link to Rosemary Palmer and Sandra Fraser who owned a couture and coffee shop in Brisbane, but that closed down.'

'Yes, that was us. We sold dresses and made coffees. It was our niche, and worked well until it closed down for a road to be built.'

Candy smiled. 'It's nearly three o'clock, Rose. An hour left, and it might all come to nothing, but at least the men around here are still enjoying themselves looking at the beautiful cars, all the beautiful women, and then there's us.'

'Hey, don't sell yourself short, Candy. We can turn heads too.'

'Well, that's the thing, we have walked past that guy about four times. He hasn't looked at you or me once, nor has he hasn't looked at the Mercedes in front of him. I mean that car looks about seventy years old, so I get that, but us? I would have thought he would look up at least once. I've been turning around to smile at him every time, but got nothing.'

'OK, this time as we go past, I'll bump into you and you bump into him. Let's see what happens. He might just be playing Fortnite waiting for his Mummy to turn up.'

As they got closer, Rose bumped, but Candy slipped and crashed into him instead. He cursed at her loudly, something about a goat and Candy's mother, and his tablet dropped to the ground. The screen cracked frozen on the last view, and he stood up. Rose bent down, picked up the tablet and went to hand it back. Then she noticed it was the bogus invoice that Callum had just sent. Nic's idiom crossed her mind: *nothing can mean everything in isolation.*

He grabbed it from her just as the view of the screen went to landscape. Rose noticed that an account number had now been populated on the bogus WORD.doc invoice. Rose looked at him, and he looked at her. 'It's you.' They both said. Wrestling the tablet from his hands, she smacked it into the top of his head.

Meantime Douglas had appeared and assisted Candy from the floor. He saw the young man attempting to wrestle the Tablet away from Rose. 'What is going on Miss Rhynge and Candy? Why is this man so angry? You did bump into him. God on earth, a young man like him, and a beautiful filly like you. You think he would be reacting quite differently.'

'He is a scammer Douglas. They intercept the invoices, change the account numbers and re-direct the

payments to themselves. You haven't paid out anything yet have you?'

'No, we're waiting for Candy to get back to us to
confirm the exchange rate.'

'Sorry Douglas, that was part of it too. There is no
Hummer. It was all a trap to catch this little fly, and
you played the spider, along with your friend Elliott.'

Douglas put his fists up and took a boxing stand.
'Then put up your dukes then you little fly. I used to
box a little when I was younger man, and live for the
day I could save a damsel in distress.'

The young man gathered his fist and smashed
it into the middle of his face, Douglas's nose was
broken, and blood began gushing from it. The older
man slumped to the floor, likely to have incurred a
broken rib too. Candy screamed and grabbed at the
younger man, but he batted her away and took off.

Rose threw her clutch at him, it missed, and he collected it from the floor. There was a lot of noise, but
no one noticed what was going on. The First Aid staff
arrived, and then an ambulance was called.

Nic and Delray came up to them. 'We thought you'd
got lost. We'd triangulated the signal to one of these
pillars. Did you guys see anything suspicious?'

Rose stepped out of the way so they could see
Douglas sprawled on the floor.

Candy had meantime sat down on the floor and was
cradling his head. 'Heroes just don't come in Army

fatigues do they, Rose? Sometimes they're dressed as a lovely old man driving a Mercedes 300SL.'

Delray bent down and asked her what that was supposed to mean. Candy shook her head, 'I'll explain it to you later.'

Rose pointed towards the side doors. 'And we found the perp too. He's trying to escape and headed over there.'

Delray and Nic took off. 'He can't get out there. The doors are locked.'

They watched as the young man was feverishly try-ing to open the locked glass doors, but they would not open. He changed direction and ran towards the front of the hall. He was still carrying his Tablet and Rose's clutch. He brushed aside the crowd waiting patiently to exit and burst into the open space. He was looking for another escape route, then he saw the Hummer.

Rose, Candy, Nic and Delray had followed him out-side, then Rose stopped and yelled out as loud as she could, 'Nic he has the keys to the Hummer. They are in my clutch. Someone get to him before he gets in a drives away.'

The young man smiled and yelled back. 'And I know it's left-hand drive. So, you can't trick me into going to the wrong side either. You dumb woman.'

Nic realised what was going on, so held out his arms so their group would slow down. They stopped and watched to see if he would fall for the ruse.

Nic began to pull the rope from the queue bollards.

'Wait Delray, just wait, but when I say go, grab two of those steel bollards. We are going to trap him inside. See the rail on the roof rack? Turn the bollard upside down, slide it through there and over the doors. He won't be able to get out. So while he is still trying to work out what's going on, take two more for the rear doors. The passenger doors are welded shut, so we don't have to worry about those.'

The man thought he had the upper hand as there was no way anyone would stand in the way of a 2-tonne truck driving at them, so he casually walked up to the left-hand door, gave a one-finger salute, unlocked the door and climbed in.

'Go, Del.'

They grabbed the bollards and rushed the truck. Nic took the left-hand driver's side, and Delray took the right. Two men nearby gathered two other bollards, and everyone slid them in place as Nic suggested. Callum and Jonty had come outside and stood there watching it all unfold. 'Is he in there Nic? His name's Billy Bakker by the way. His mother must be around somewhere too, most likely in the Commodore, wondering what's going on.'

'Yep, to all that.'

The man in the Hummer realised he had been out-maneuvered, as muffled profanities were coming from inside, along with the occasional fist into the roof and door panel. Nic called everybody to attention. 'Listen, he's not going anywhere. There is no engine in the

Hummer. It's a shell. It won't start, so please step away and we'll let the Police take it from here.'

Everyone clapped.

Not far away in the Convention Centre carpark, Mar Bakker was wondering what had happened to Billy. It was getting late and she was still suspicious of all the invoices coming through as a WORD.doc. Billy had said it was likely that the US was not used to doing business in Australia, but she could not convince him to be more careful. She also knew this would have to be their last play, and was concerned that only the new online ING bank account held all the money at the moment. Billy had said it all has to come out slowly though, so the Banks wouldn't get suspicious.

Damn those banks, and she smiled.

She heard the 4.30 news come on the local radio station. The headline story was about a young man refusing to come out of a Hummer that was parked out the front of the Adelaide Motor Show. The newsreader could not hold back his laughter when he read out his next line. 'Well listeners, Billy Bakker should have checked that it had an engine before he tried to carjack it. The Police are there now just waiting for him to come out.'

Damn it Billy. We had to go one more time, didn't we?

There was a noise down in the carpark entrance, so she decided to get out of the car and take a look. Perhaps it was Billy after all. However, it *was* the Police.

There was a woman and a man with them too, and Mar recognized she was one of the women from the other day. *Those two women were just taking a selfie. Surely, they didn't take pictures of the car when Billy tried to run them down.*

Mar stepped back into the Commodore, driver's side this time, and the posse was coming closer. It was now or never, so she turned the engine over and drove out of the space acting as casually as possible, even giving a polite nod to the police. She put the card in the slot and the arm slowly rose. Mar put her foot on the pedal and was almost free, but the lights changed to red. It was then she heard a shout that she had been dreading; 'That's her in the car, Nic.'

Mar saw the police run towards her car, so she started nudging the car in front, then swung around it, planted her foot and was out. Glancing to the right, as she was about to cross the traffic, she pushed the accelerator and lurched across the gap. There was a large looming shadow in the passenger window, it was a tram.

It smashed into the side of her car, pushing her about 150 metres, and her car collided with a pylon under the Morphett Street Bridge. Mar thought she heard something just before she slipped into the black abyss. 'Hello, Mar Bakker. My name is Nic Thorn, and you are under a citizen's arrest.'

CHAPTER 19

Monday. Nic, Rose and the Team met with the South Australian Police, and the cross border Police Teams were skyped in. The Commissioner summarised the case:

"The death of Marilyn Ann Bakker had been ruled an accident. The State of NSW will arrange for her body to be shipped back to Griffith. Wilhelm (Billy) Bakker was now incarcerated, pending the finalisation of the charges. The ING Bank account used on the bogus invoices held nearly one and a half million dollars and will be recovered from the Bank, subject to the appropriate subpoenas.'

After they wound up, Nic's Team met back at one of the conference rooms at the Intercontinental Hotel. There were handshakes and back-slapping all around. Even Driver had driven up from Victor Harbor for the session, but the biggest cheer was for Delray and Candy. Nic was true to his word, as he presented them with the $5,000 bonus.

The party broke up, they waved off Driver, which left Nic and Rose alone. 'Dinner, Rose? There is a great Spanish BBQ Restaurant just up the road, La Boca.' Rose nodded. 'Sure. Nic, but before you cross the street take my hand.'

Nic smiled. 'Life is what happens while you're making other plans. That's a quote from Alan Saunders, January 1957.'

Rose shook her head. 'No Nic, it's from John Lennon, December 1980. Have you heard of him?' He punched her softly in the arm.

'So what's next for us Nic?'

'We are off to Pinnaroo tomorrow, but tonight I am hanging out for a famous South Australian delicacy, the Pie Floater. It's a Balfour's meat pie served on a bed of mushy green peas.'

Rose looked at him. 'Don't forget the tomato sauce.'

It was 5.00 a.m. and Nic's mobile phone rang. He grabbed at it and with bleary eyes, wondered who would be ringing at this early hour.

'Morning Nic. It's Rose. Wakey, wakey. You said we have an early start today.'

Nic lay back on the bed. 'Five o'clock is not an early start. It's the middle of the night, and how did you get this number?'

'I rang your sister.'

'No, you didn't. Who gave it to you?'

'Your Sister Gwen, the nun.'

'When did you meet her?'

'Facebook,'

'She doesn't do Facebook, nor would have she given it to you.'

There was a pause. 'I have my ways, Nic. You have taught me well, sensei.'

'Are you always this chipper at this time of the morning, Rose?'

'Yes, but not on the days that end in 'y' as the others make me sad.'

'Rose.'

'Yes, Nic.'

'I am going to hang up now and remember, like most Hotels the checkout time is ten a.m. So, go back to sleep and I will meet you at the breakfast parlour at eight. We'll check out after that like normal people, so it's goodnight from me.' He waited for her response and waited, then he realised she had hung up. 'Damn you, Rose.'

They met for breakfast, checked out, and went across the road to hire a car for the Pinnaroo investigation. Nic was pushing Rose's two suitcases and she had his smaller carry-on. 'What's in here then?'

Rose smiled. 'The stuff we didn't need. Sandy only took a carry-on, and besides that, what happened to your massive backpack, the little computer bag, and where are your business suits?'

'The big bag was Drivers, and that bag you had was inside it. There was nothing in the computer bag apart from newspapers and a balloon. As for my suits,

I hire them from Peter Shearers in Rundle Mall. It's all about the image.'

'But what about those ghastly, red Patent leather loafers?'

'They're mine, and my sister bought them for me.'

'Oops, sorry Nic.'

They presented themselves at the AVIS desk and the only car available was a white RS Commodore. Rose smiled. 'How ironic, a 'cut and shut'

'Too early Rose, and be nice. She was Billy's' mother after all. Besides how do you know about that type of Insurance scam?'

The desk clerk looked at her. 'We certainly do not 'cut and shut', young lady.' Nic asked Rose to hand over her Business Credit Card, and the paperwork was completed in her name, with Nic as a nominated driver.

'Are you over twenty five Miss Rhynge? I need to see your driver's license too please.'

Rose looked at Nic and wondered how this would work. 'Please hand him your Driver's license, Rosie.'

Rose handed it over and the clerk read it, then remarked that it was in a different name: "*Rosemary Palmer.*"

Nic interjected, explaining that Rhynge was her married name and she had not yet changed the license. He seemed to accept that and finalised everything, but as he was handing back her card held it back, and again mentioned her name. 'Hey, you're married name is Rhynge-Rosie. My wife's Norwegian. Ringa-Rosie that's funny. I bet you get that all the time.'

Rose shrugged. 'And that's why I'm keeping my name.'

Nic accepted the keys and they headed to the car. Rose commented, 'At least he called me a young lady, and wanted to know if I was over twenty-five. That's something, after all, Candy thought I was forty."

'Yep, too true. Anyhow, we have to make a stop off along the way. It's just at the end of the street at the Royal Adelaide Hospital. We're catching up with Douglas, as he is being dismissed this morning. The nose was broken, but the ribs were only bruised, so they were allowing him to go home. Elliott is picking him up in their new car.'

'Surely they're not driving a million-dollar Mercedes around Adelaide?'

'Not the Merc no, but you will see.'

They drove down North Terrace onto Port Road, took the right-hand turn into the hospital, and found a carpark. Douglas was waiting for them in the foyer. Rose gave him a hug trying very carefully to avoid his nose. His eyes were bruised blackened circles, and Nic smiled. Douglas gingerly touched his nose checking it was still there.

Nic opened his phone. 'I assume that you've seen the clip on the net of Miss Panda-Eyes at GOMA in Brisbane?'

'Yes, Elliott showed me, that poor little filly, dripping

wet like that. Mascara running and those round black panda eyes. Why?'

'Well, would you like a photo standing with Miss Panda-Eyes? One for the family album.' They posed, and Nic took the photo.

Douglas looked at Rose. 'That was you?'

Rose shrugged. 'Yes, not one of my better moments.'

Douglas nodded. 'Another successful ruse with our Mr. Thyme/Thorn then?'

'Yes, I guess so.'

They walked him out to the patient collection area, and a Hummer was coming up the ramp. It stopped next to them, looking huge on the small road. Elliott stepped out, walked around and kissed Douglas on the side of his face. Douglas stood there dumbstruck. 'What's this then? And whose is it?'

Nic looked at him. 'It's yours, Douglas. It does have some miles on it and it's not exactly new. We think you deserve it for taking a punch in the face for us.'

'I can't take this. It's too much.'

This time Rose stepped up to him and kissed him on the other cheek. 'At least accept it from a distressed damsel then.' He tried to smile at Nic and Rose but winced from the pain. 'Thank you, and I will. And next time I see a damsel in distress I won't stick my nose into their business. Getting punched in the old proboscis is a trite too painful.'

Elliott assisted him into the Hummer and drove off.

Nic and Rose returned to the Commodore. Nic laid the phones on the console to link them to the car's Bluetooth, and they headed off. The plan was to drive directly to Pinnaroo with an expected arrival around 3 p.m.

'That was nice, Nic. I mean an incredible gesture, but nice.'

'It was your idea. You reminded me of the insane profit I made on the sale of the Mercedes SL, and I felt it was the right thing to do for Douglas. Especially since he has bought four cars from me already in the last three years. All over five hundred thousand too. Sometimes I do need a reality check, so thanks for that.'

'Well, speaking of cheques. When do I get paid?'

'Mm, let me think about that a bit longer.'

'And on that Nic, how do you get paid?'

'Well, let's just say, like in this invoicing caper, the Insurance Underwriters have already paid out on the claims and written off the loss, so anything they recover is a hundred per cent profit to them. Here, it looks like it is around two million, with most of it still sitting in the ING Bank Account. I usually get around ten per cent of the Gross amount recovered, plus expenses. Sometimes, I receive reward payouts from the AFP or the local police. For the little jobs like this Pinnaroo one, well that's just a flat fee.'

'OK, I think I get that, but how do you let them know your fees for service?'

'I invoice them.'

'That's funny Nic. So you had a vested interest in tracking these scammers down then? Do you mean they also managed to get one past the Great Nic Thorn?'

'Not me, but some people that I do business with and that disappointed me, but let's not talk about that as we have hours of my music to listen to on the way.'

Rose smiled. 'Nothing sounds better than listening to Kenny G blaring out his little sassy brass honker, barreling down the highway at a hundred clicks.'

'Rose, Rose, I have something even better, and as a testament to the recently departed Mar Bakker, I have a collection from Boney M, the Disco group from the late seventies: 'Brown Girl in The Ring', 'Rasputin', and their greatest hit that never was, 'Ma Baker.''

'Nic, can I ask you something really serious?'

Nic hesitated. 'OK, I think.'

Rose grinned. 'Just how old are you?'

'Ma Baker' was played, and Nic put it on repeat again twice straight away. Rose had been bopping along and then looked at him. 'Gee Nic, a lot of their songs sound the same, don't they?'

'As opposed to the songs of Kenny G that we've just finished listening to?'

Rose leaned over and turned the sound system off. 'How about we have it quiet for a while, and please let me know if you'd like me to drive.' Rose then promptly fell asleep and snored just a tiny little bit. Nic smiled and stored that in his memory for later.

Just under three hours later, they pulled into the BP at Pinnaroo and he stopped the engine. Rose woke and stretched. 'Damn, are we only at? ...Are we there yet? Do you need me to drive now?'

'We're at Pinnaroo, Rose.'

'Oh, right, err quick question if I may. Where are we going to stay? Is there a Marriott or at least a Stamford Plaza? I am happy to shout.' Rose offered up her Business Credit Card.

'Don't worry, I have set that up already given I could not trust you to remain in your hotel in Adelaide. I am at the Pinnaroo Hotel, and you are at the Pinnaroo Motel. I know, confusing right, two lodgings with almost the same names?'

'So, what's the scoop here? Are we going to hang around and wait for a truck full of bottles and cans to drive past, and chase them back to Adelaide?'

'Not quite. I've had my spies working overtime, and the scoop is that there is a shipment due in a couple of days. So, we have a free evening to see the sights and the shops of downtown Pinnaroo. We'll be pooped after that, and will need an early night.'

'But I'm bright-eyed and bushy-tailed, I need the rush, the nightlife, and the Pinnaroo experience.'

'That's because you slept for two hours, and by the way, you snore.'

'That's not nice. I haven't had any complaints

before, well none that were as rude as you are, and anyway, I'm glad that we have separate rooms. I won't have to listen to you talk in your sleep.'

'Separate rooms Rose, in separate Hotels, on separate streets too.'

Rose nodded. 'Yes, there is that, but sometimes walls have ears. Remember that.' Nic filled up the car with petrol, disposed of the lunch rubbish, and drove around the town looking at the sights. It didn't take long.

Then they drove to the border crossing, about five kilometres from the town and stepped out of the car. There was a small Besser brick hut, with a sign on the door that showed:

"Opening hours 8 am to 8 pm – closed for lunch between 12-1."

As the booth was manned, Nic walked over to introduce himself to the Border Officer. 'G'day. I'm Nic Fury, and we are here on behalf of the South Australian Environmental Protection Authority. We've been authorised to investigate the cross-border transporting of recyclables for illegal refunds.'

The man nodded. 'Gillen Green, Border Officer, but everyone calls me "Baggy". Nothing much gets past me with that sort of thing.'

Rose interjected. 'Sorry Mr Baggy, as the opening times are shown on the sign, isn't there a chance they could come through before eight a.m. and after eight p.m. or when you're closed for lunch?'

The officer looked at her. "We country folk are an honest bunch, and I suspect you're not from around here.'

'Well, Nic is. He was born in Ouyen and his sister lives on a farm in…' Nic quickly interrupted her. 'Now Rosie, what have I bin tellin' ya about talking about my kin-folk?'

Rose looked at Nic and realised she shouldn't have mentioned his background.

Nic continued: 'It's happened before Baggy. There was a case up near Willaston a couple of years ago. The EPA fined the guy five grand for trying to bring in forty-five thousand drink containers. His truck broke down, he got caught, and that was the end of it.'

Baggy nodded. 'I heard that one too, but nothing that exciting happens around here, Mr Fury. Anyway, I'm closing up now to have some dinner before the six o'clock rush hour starts. We can get up to four cars in a row sometimes you know.'

Nic shook his hand. 'Thank you for your time; then nodded at Rose. 'It's tucker time for us too. Let's get back to Pinnaroo.'

They returned to their car, and Nic continued once they were inside. 'I've heard this recycling thing has something to do with the sports field at Murrayville. It's a town just over the border, in Victoria. The locals play both footy, baseball and cricket there, and I've just met Baggy Green who happens to work on the border.'

'Yes, but why is that interesting? And sorry about the sister thing, I am not good at all this secret squirrel stuff as yet.'

'A "Baggy Green" is a cricketer's cap, and don't sell yourself short, Rose, you did give Billy Bakker a smash on the noggin. We are batting two for two with our jobs so far.' And with that comment, he touched her nose with his forefinger.

'Please don't do that, it makes my nose twitch like Samantha's from Bewitched, and I could turn you into a frog if I wanted to. Ribbitt.'

They arrived at Nic's hotel, ate dinner, and afterwards, he walked her to her hotel.

CHAPTER 20

With no plans until around noon, they both agreed to sleep in until nine. Rose walked over to Nic's Hotel, but the car was gone. *Damn it Nic, where are you?*

Rose now had his mobile number, pulled out her phone, and scrolled through to the 'N's' but his number was gone. Then, flicking through the rest of the numbers saw a new listing at 'P' under the name Panda-Eyes. Rose looked at it, thought it was Nic's, and called the number. Nic answered, and Rose could hear the engine noise.

'Damn it Nic, where are you? We were going to meet for breakfast. The bakery does a great egg and bacon muffin, and you promised to take me there.'

'Sorry Rose, something came up early this morning. I had to take a run over the border to check it out. Everything is up in the air at the moment.'

Rose considered his comment. 'Are you in a plane?' She waited for a response, but another voice came through her phone:

'This is Bravo, Delta, Delta Confirming a Mayday.'

Rose took a breath. 'Where are you Nic?'

'We are currently heading west over Parilla, towards the Lameroo Hospital.'

'What's happening?'

'Baggy rang me late last night and asked me if I'd like to meet him at his farm over the border. He offered to take me up in his crop duster early this morning for an aerial view of things. Sorry, but it's only a two-seater, but we didn't quite make it to Murrayville, and are now heading west to Lameroo.'

'And?'

'Well, he's called in a Mayday. He was booked in to have his gallbladder removed at the hospital tomorrow, but the little tyke wants to make an appearance today.'

The second voice again came through Rose's phone: 'Have you flown before Mr Fury? I think I'm going to be closing my eyes now. I'm not feeling too good.'

Nic responded. 'Yep, I'm RPL certified to fly one of these and sorry, Rose, I'll be hanging up now. Can you get someone to drive you to Lameroo and collect me?'

Rose responded. 'But I don't know anyone here?'

Baggy called out: 'The Pinnaroo Ambulance will be driving down from Lameroo to meet us. Their Ambo station is on Railway Terrace South. The guy in charge is called Plugger. He's the local plumber.'

Nic came back onto the call. 'Right, that's settled. See you there.' He hung up.

Rose quickly headed off toward the Ambulance Station and met with the Senior Ambulance Officer.

'Are you Plugger? A Mayday has been called in by Gillen Green. He's currently flying to the Lameroo Hospital.'

The officer looked at Rose. 'Yes, I'm Senior Officer Leake...but who's Gillen Green?'

Rose shrugged. 'Sorry, I meant Baggy. He suggested I could catch a ride with you, and meet them there.'

Plugger nodded. 'Oh right, Baggy...but who are them?'

'My business partner...Nic ..um... Fury is flying the plane. I just spoke to him on the phone.' Plugger shook his head. 'Baggy doesn't like other people flying his plane.'

Rose nodded. 'Well, it's an emergency. Baggy mentioned his gallbladder.'

'Oh, that's right. It's coming out tomorrow. The first one is always early.'

Rose looked at him. 'I think that applies to babies, not gallbladders. How long will the drive take?'

'It's about thirty k's, so normally under half an hour, but we can use the lights, sirens and everything, so it could take a little less.'

Rose considered his response. 'Can I ride with you then?'

Plugger nodded. 'Sure, but you'll have to sit in the back. Our regular passengers are usually not so talkative, and are lying down.'

A second Ambulance officer approached them. 'Hi, I'm Maddie Winter, you must be Rose. I've just got off the phone from the Doctor at Lameroo. They've made space for Baggy to be operated on this afternoon.' Maddie looked at her watch. 'The plane is expected to land in about twenty minutes, and they're mowing the paddock at the back of the hospital for the landing.'

In less than twenty minutes the Ambulance arrived at the paddock, and they were waiting for Nic to bring the plane down. Maddie shielded her eyes from the sun and pointed to the plane. 'It's going to be a rough landing.'

Rose nodded. 'I'm sure Nic knows what he's doing.'

'Has he done this sort of thing before?'

Rose nodded. 'Well, he seems to have everything else he does under control, so I suspect he knows how to land a plane.'

They watched the plane make its approach. It went a little sideways, then gracefully touched down. The passenger door opened, and then Plugger and Maddie raced over to them with a gurney. They put Baggy in the Ambulance and drove off to the hospital. Nic moved around from the other side of the plane and approached Rose. 'Well, what did you think of that?'

Rose shrugged. 'I guess it's just part of other stuff that you know how to do.'

Nic grinned. 'Flying is easy, landing is hard.'

Rose nodded again. 'Um...slight hole in your plan.'

Nic was puzzled. 'What's that, Rose?'

'How do we get back to Pinnaroo?'

Nic grinned. 'I've still got the keys to the plane.

So, how would you like me to show you the sights of Lameroo, Pinnaroo and Murrayville, all from the comfort of the plane, with your friendly pilot, Nic.'

'I'd rather wait for Maddie and Plugger. I assume they'll be going back to Pinnaroo. There'll be room for me in the back.'

Nic shrugged, secured the plane and they walked over to the Hospital where Maddie was re-stocking the Ambulance. 'That was a good landing, Mr Fury.'

'Call me, Nic.'

'OK, that was a good landing, Nic. How long have you been flying?'

'A while. I don't own a plane, but have to keep my hours up, so I fly whenever someone is happy to let me.' Maddie nodded. 'Baggy mentioned you're here with the EPA to investigate a cross-border recycling thing.'

Nic smiled. 'But don't tell anyone, it's supposed to be a secret.'

Maddy shook her head. 'This is the county, Nic. There are no secrets.'

'Well, this one needs to be kept on the down-low. My sources tell me that something is going on at Murrayville.' Maddie grinned. 'You mean the green grass on the oval?'

Nic nodded again. 'Yep, something like that. Do you know anything about it?'

'Not really, but there's a cricket game there

tomorrow. We'll be on duty in case someone cops one in the head from a wayward bouncer.'

'Good to know, thanks, Maddie. What time does it start?'

'Should be around ten.'

Rose looked at Maddie. 'Will we need entry tickets?'

'Nope, but everyone will know you're there. Strangers in town, that sort of thing.'

Nic nodded again. 'OK, we'll see you there, and Maddie, when are you heading back to Pinnaroo? Rose would like a lift if that's OK.'

Maddie looked at Rose. 'Are you sure you don't want to fly back? Baggy told me to let Nic know to fly the plane back to his farm. Otherwise, it will have to stay here until he fully recovers from the op. It could be weeks before he's allowed to fly it again.'

Rose nodded. 'If it's not too much to ask, I'd like a ride back with you. I don't like flying in those little rattlers, I prefer my planes with reclining seats, free drinks and in-house movies.'

Nic looked at Rose. 'I didn't know you didn't like flying.'

Rose shrugged, and Maddie nodded. 'All good from me. Plugger lives here in Lameroo, so I'll be on my own anyway. It will be good to have a chat with someone else for a change.' Rose and Maddie climbed into the Ambulance, gave Nic a wave, and headed off toward Pinnaroo, whilst Nic entered the hospital.

Rose and Maddie were about ten minutes into the return trip when a call came through that there had been a car accident at the B12/B57 highway intersection. Maddie lifted the two-way. 'Five minutes ETA.' She turned to Rose. 'Have you ...um...what's your background? Have you done any re-sus stuff?'

Rose sighed. 'No, I'm ...well, sure, let me know what I can do to help.'

Maddie nodded. 'It could be bad, but we won't know what it is until we get there, it's a notorious site for accidents.'

The sirens were turned on, Maddie stepped on the accelerator and in less than five minutes were at the accident site where a car had driven through the intersection. It was parked up against Spinifex grass. Maddie climbed quickly from the ambulance. 'This is Donny Blucher's car. I'm going to need you to follow my instructions. Don't think just do. Can you do that?'

Rose nodded. 'Yes.'

'Good, grab the red 'jump' bag from the back and I'll see what's going on.'

Rose moved to the rear of the Ambulance and removed the bag, then ran around to find Maddie. She was already calling out for her. 'Can you get the defib machine instead? It's a yellow box with a blue square. It's on the wall.'

Rose ran back, located the box and meantime, Maddie had opened the car door, and was leaning in at the driver. 'Have you been taking your pills, Donny? You know you're not supposed to be driving.' The driver's head had lolled sideways in the seat. 'I need the box, Rose. Stat.'

Rose returned with the defibrillator and began unclipping the sides of the box. 'Good job.' Maddie prepared the unit and clipped the points onto Donny's chest. 'Stand back, Rose. I'm about to hit him with the charge. He has bradycardia, his heart slows down. He shouldn't be driving. One, two, three.' The machine jolted and Donny's chest heaved. 'Come on, Donny. Not out here. Let's get your heart beating properly.' The man's eyes fluttered, then he took a couple of deep breaths, opened his eyes, and smiled. 'Hi Maddie, we shouldn't keep meeting like this.'

Maddie sighed. 'Donny, I'm going to move you and we are going to take you to Lameroo for observation. Are you OK for me to do that? Can you walk?'

Donny nodded, slowly stepped from the car and they assisted him to the ambulance. 'My arrhythmia will be the death of me one day. Can you take my car back? I'll need it to get to the cricket match tomorrow.'

Maddie shook her head. 'I don't think you'll be going tomorrow. You have at least a couple of days in hospital before you can be discharged. Stop scaring us like this. I'll get someone to collect the car tomorrow.'

'Damn, I guess the game will be one umpire short.'

Donny then looked at Rose. 'Hi, I'm Donny. Are you single or married?'

Rose nodded. 'I'm single, but I think you're too young for me.'

Donny smiled softly as they lay him on the gurney 'I'm only sixty-five, but still young at heart.' Maddie attached a nasal cannula, stepped through to the driver's seat and called the hospital on the two-way. 'Rose, can you stay back there with him and let me know if his condition changes.'

Rose had just taken her seat when her phone rang. 'Hi Nic, thanks for letting me know. I'm heading back to Lameroo with Maddie. We had to attend to an incident on the highway. I'm fine, but we'll be a little late returning to Pinnaroo tonight. I'll see you at the hospital.'

Donny was listening to the call. 'Is Nic your boyfriend?'

Rose smiled. 'No, well I'm not sure, but I think you should worry about getting better, not about me.'

Maddie did a U-turn in the ambulance and they headed back to Lameroo. 'Thanks for your help. You did very well. A lot of people can't keep a clear head.'

Rose nodded 'Thanks, I've been working with Nic for a while. He keeps me on my toes.'

Maddie nodded. 'How long has it been?'

'What's the date now?

'The fifteenth, I think.'

Rose sighed. 'Well, if you can keep a secret. It's only been a couple of weeks.'

Maddie grinned. 'So, is he your boyfriend.'

'I...um...the truth is I have no idea what he is.'

It took them less than ten minutes to return to Lameroo Hospital, and Nic was waiting out the front for them to arrive. He had been visiting Baggy Green. Rose stepped from the ambulance and approached him. 'That was exciting, but please remind me never to grow old.'

The hospital crew assisted Maddie with Donny, and she returned a few moments later with a young boy. 'This is my grandson, Jack, he's been visiting my mother in the Aged Care Centre. I'll take him back home with me, Rose, you will have to fly back with Nic. The back of the ambulance is a bit of a mess.'

The boy was squirming a little and looked up to his Grandmother. 'Can we go home now, and can we use the sirens?'

Maddie nodded. 'Sure. I just want to thank Miss Palmer and Mr Fury for helping me save Donny and Baggy.' The boy sighed, moved away from them, and opened a comic book he was holding.

'Thanks again, Nic, and Rose, you were really helpful. When we meet again at the cricket tomorrow, I'll shout you a couple of coffees.'

Nic nodded. 'Not a problem, glad we could help. We'd better go, it's getting late and I still have to fly back to Baggy's farm to collect the car.' The boy overheard the comment and looked up at his mother. 'Is like he a real superhero?' Can he fly?'

Maddie smiled. 'In a plane, Jack.'

'Oh, it's just that you said his name was Nick Fury.' The boy held up his comic book. 'It says here that Nic Fury is the Head of Shield, and looks after all The Avengers.'

Rose looked at Nic. 'I think we'd better get going.'

Nic squatted down to shake the boy's hand. 'You know Jack, The Avengers only exist in comic books and movies. The real superheroes are Ambulance Officers like your Grandmother. They wear uniforms and save people every day.'

Rose looked at Nic. 'Hey, you re-cycled the quote I said to Candy.'

'Yep, sometimes I steal stuff too, but usually it's only good ideas.'

They waved goodbye to Maddie and Jack, then headed to the plane. As they climbed in Nic handed Rose a couple of pills. 'Maddie gave them to me for your anxiety.'

Rose shrugged. 'Thanks, but no thanks, I'll be OK. How long is the flight?'

Nic put the pills in his pocket, began his pre-flight checks and put his headphones on, then gestured to Rose to do the same. His voice came through. 'About thirty minutes. Meanwhile, we can listen to some music, sometimes that can assist as a distraction.'

Rose looked around the cockpit. 'I can't see a radio.'

Nic smiled and started singing the theme song from the 1965 film, Those Magnificent Men in Their Flying Machine. Rose told him to stop.

Less than thirty minutes later, they were landing on Baggy's airstrip and Rose finally started breathing normally. They collected the car and drove back to Pinnaroo.

CHAPTER 21

It was around nine a.m. when Nic met Rose at her hotel and they were deciding what to do next. Nic checked his watch. 'Can you grab a couple of muffins for breakfast and meet me at the Library in Bundey Terrace? Ask someone if you need directions.'

Rose walked off to find breakfast. Bought coffee with muffins, and as they would not take payment by card for less than $10, also bought a couple of yeast buns. Nic was already at the library when Rose arrived. He was leaning against the car and she took a picture without him noticing, just for her family album, and then handed over the breakfast.

Nic took a bite of his muffin and placed it on the car. 'We need to check out the names of the current Murrayville Cricketers and Footballers to see if there's a link. Something is going on as the club seems to have recently come into money, nothing major, but the grass on the oval is lush and green. I'm wondering how they afford to keep it watered.'

Rose nodded. 'Nothing means nothing until it means something doesn't it, oh great sensei?'

Nic grinned. 'After we finish breakfast can you go into the library, and ask for Tiffany? See if you can find the AGM minutes for the two clubs for the last five years, photocopy them and meet me out here in about thirty minutes. If I am not here don't panic, as I have to go back to the BP to check something out.'

Rose nodded, and Nic continued: 'It's a date then, Rose.'

'No Nic, it's a job remember? Boy, you're lucky you have me around to keep you from forgetting stuff. It must be the senility creeping in, being over forty.'

Nic shook his head. 'I'm thirty-six, Rose, and I would tell you my date of birth, but then you'd spoil me with presents and cake. Too much muffin keeps you puffin'.'

They finished breakfast. Nic noticed the yeast buns and grinned. 'I hope we don't eat them before the cricket game starts.' Nic opened the library door for Rose, then returned to the car and drove away.

Rose located Tiffany and photocopied the minutes after convincing her she was from the State Gaming Commission. Rose was going through the list of names and noticed Nic had already returned and was waiting outside.

'Did you find anything, Rose?'

'I think so, and I found something out from Tiffany too, but it's not in the minutes. Baggy used to be the President of the Cricket Club, but he recently re-signed due to a disagreement. The Treasurer, Wade, is now both Treasurer and Acting President of the amalgamated Committee. Baggy wanted the two clubs to remain separate, but as farm numbers have dwindled, there were fewer Committee members around. Geoff Markin, the Secretary, retired to Adelaide and the green-keeper has...well, I didn't find that out. It must make it difficult to run a local club if you're the only one to sign the cheques, and an interesting meeting if there are any objections raised or points of order."

'All that in half an hour? That's good work.'

Rose nodded. 'Oh, and by the way, the photocopying cost a hundred dollars. I sort of accidentally on purpose, added the extra zero. I thought the Library could do with some new books.'

It was around ten o'clock when they arrived at the Murrayville Oval. The teams were warming up, throwing balls, catching balls and avoiding the angry bull in the adjacent paddock. A rubble road surrounded the oval, so they were able to park the car facing the game.

Nic jumped the fence and plucked a sample of the green grass, chewed on it, and then spat it out. 'This looks and tastes like wheatgrass, it's no wonder the cows are so healthy around here. Anyway, please stay in the car, Rose. I'm going to go for a little walk to see if I can find out what is going on. Try to remain inconspicuous. We are strangers in the town, and country folk don't like strangers. There are binoculars in the glove box if you want to use them.' Rose watched him go, then took out the binoculars and watched him go some more.

The game was about to start, the toss had been won by the local team, and they had elected to bowl. The umpires moved into position and Rose noticed something familiar about the shape of the umpire at square leg. Rose focused the binoculars and realised it was Nic, although he was disguised under a large white bucket hat and large white coat.

Rose shook her head and muttered: 'I don't think being an umpire is remaining inconspicuous Nic.'

The first over was a wicketless maiden, despite the fielding team appealing several times for leg-before-wicket. It was now Nic's turn to attend to the bowler's end. Nic called "No ball' at the first delivery. Rose shook her head again. 'Way to go, Nic. Now you have the whole fielding team looking at you, and everybody in the crowd watching the game.'

The bowler remonstrated with Nic, then stormed back his mark to make the next delivery. It too was called a "No ball."

Rose decided to get out of the car for a better view and stood alongside the people parked next to her. The third ball was delivered, and "No ball," was called again, and by this time it was all getting rather testy. Rose nodded towards the commotion on the field. 'What's going on?'

One of the spectators looked at Rose. 'My son is the bowler, and he is throwing the ball as his elbow is bent too far. He's always been a bit of a chucker, and they've got stricter on this rule recently. It looks like he's still using his old action.'

'What happens if he can't bowl properly?'

The man moved closer to the fence and yelled out. 'Hey ump, just let him finish the over.' He turned back to Rose. 'I hate it when they use out-of-town umpires. If Donny was here, he'd let it go.'

Rose nodded. 'Donny is in Lameroo Hospital. He had a bit of a heart attack.'

'So I heard, and you're the helper that helped Maddie get him to the hospital.' Rose shrugged. 'I didn't do anything, just followed her instructions.'

The man nodded. 'Good job anyway, but we need him back ASAP. Hopefully, he can replace this umpire.' Rose nodded. 'Do you know who the umpire is?

The man shook his head 'No idea, but he needs to pull his head in so the game can re-start.' Rose tried to hold back a laugh. 'Can I ask you another question?'

'Sure.'

Rose pointed to the grass. 'Why is it so green? I thought there was a water shortage out this way.'

The man shrugged. 'There is sort of, but um...I really don't know. There were major earthworks between the end of footy and cricket starting. Someone said underground sprinklers had been installed, but no one knows where the controls are, or where the money came from. There used to be bores drilled down to the water table, but it all got too expensive, so they stopped pumping it up.'

The cricketers took their positions again. 'Oh, good it looks like it's going to restart.' He called out. 'Howzat!' as the team had appealed for a catch. It was given out, and the crowd cheered.

Rose returned to the car and happened to notice a man on the other side of the field. He was dressed in a high-vis jacket and looking around as if he was trying to avoid anybody watching him. Rose raised the binoculars to see what he was up to. He went up to a rubbish bin next to the changerooms, lifted it, placed it on the ground and then opened a panel underneath. Suddenly, the pop-up sprinklers popped up, and water began spraying out from them. The players tried to keep playing, but the field was now water-logged and the pitch was unplayable.

The game was abandoned.

Rose watched Nic to see what he would do next. He sat down and waited for the others to leave the oval. Rose stepped under the fence rail and walked over to him. 'I thought we were supposed to be inconspicuous. How does being an umpire, and calling out the bowler for throwing, be inconspicuous?'

Nic shrugged. 'I thought I'd get as close as I could to the source of the truth, but as it turned out, these guys had no idea about the green grass either. No one appears to know.' Rose helped him stand. 'Or they're keeping it a secret.'

'I don't think so, they just seemed to be genuinely pleased they have a better surface to play on.'

Rose nodded. 'I think I saw something though. There was a guy over by the changerooms, he lifted one of the rubbish bins and there appeared to be a panel underneath it. I think that was the controls for the sprinklers.'

'How did you see that?'

Rose grinned. 'With the binoculars, you told me to keep an eye on things, so I did.'

Nic nodded. 'Well, I found out something at the BP Service Station too. A local truck often passes through around lunchtime with the sides and top covered by a canvas canopy.'

'Why is that suspicious?'

'This is a farming area, and everyone knows the sides need to be kept open for the animals to breathe.'

Rose looked at him. 'But what if they're carrying cereals and stuff?' Nic grinned. 'Boy, you ask a lot of questions. Anyway, show me where this bin is.'

They moved from the oval and Rose headed toward the bin. 'He lifted it, and there should be a panel underneath.' Nic looked at it, then wrapped his arms around the container and gave it a pull. Nothing happened. 'Maybe I should have had more Wheaties for breakfast this morning.' He tried again, with the same result. Rose stepped around the bin and noticed two padlocks holding the bin in place. It was attached to a cement platform 'Maybe there's more to it?'

Nic kicked the bin and something clicked. Rose looked at the dent in the side of the bin. 'Now you've done it. You'll have to pay for the damage.'

Nic licked the palm of his hand and rubbed the dent. 'There, good as new. We'll leave it, and try plan B at the BP.'

Rose nodded. 'What's plan B?'

'We need to find out from the locals who has the equipment and knowledge to install an underground sprinkler system whilst no one was looking.'

CHAPTER 22

The following morning they were driving back to Murrayville. Nic set the cruise control. 'My spies tell me that one of the farmers owns a tractor, and was seen with a modified plough attachment.'

'Don't most farmers own tractors?'

'Well, when pulled along, this one creates a furrow around the size of an agriculture pipe, which is about the size you'd need if you were installing an underground watering system.'

'Is that where we're heading now?'

'Yep, but I have to tell you, the property is next door to my sisters, so if you see someone that looks like me in a dress, don't say anything.'

'Wow, so it's finally happening, you're introducing me to your family.'

'Not really, I haven't seen her for ages, so I don't know what she looks like anymore.' Nic noticed a car passing them, and he waived. 'That could've been her in that car.'

Rose turned her head. 'Damn, I missed the details

on the registration plate. I think it was a white Holden Rodeo, so I'll know what to look for next time.'

'Nope, it wasn't her. She drives a white Holden Triton.'

'Nic, Mitsubishi make the Triton, not Holden.'

'Well, it definitely wasn't her then.'

After about fifteen minutes, Nic slowed the car down, turned off the highway and they drove through a farm gate. Rose looked around at the property. 'Who's place is this?' Nic nodded. 'The man with the furrow attachment thing that he tows behind his tractor.'

Rose sighed. 'Are we supposed to be in here?'

'Probably not, but they're not expecting us. It's rude if you drive up someone's driveway and don't get out of your car. It's a country thing.' Nic pulled the car to a stop, turned off the engine but didn't get out of the vehicle. 'Maybe they're not home.'

Rose leaned over and pressed the horn. 'I would say you're right. Are we still going to get out of the car?'

Nic nodded. 'We have to, they might not have seen us, or they could be injured or something, and be trapped inside the house.'

Rose opened her door and Nic stepped out of his side. 'I think we'd better look around.' Rose shook her head. 'If you're looking for a tractor with a plough thing, they wouldn't keep it by the house, it would be in a machinery shed.'

Nic nodded. 'Yep, I'd say you're right, so let's walk

down to the sheds.' Nic started to walk towards an old, corrugated iron shed. 'There could be something in here that we need to look at.' Nic went to the shed door and tried the handle. It opened, so he stepped inside. 'I think I found something.'

Rose followed behind him. 'What?'

'The Ark of the Covenant.'

'No, you didn't. Indiana found it. I saw that at the movies.'

'So, you know Harrison Ford from that movie but didn't know he was in Star Wars? He flew the Millennium Falcon with Chewbacca.'

Rose looked at him. No, he didn't, it was a Pan Am Clipper, and I still don't understand how he missed the German spy sitting across the aisle in the plane.'

Nic shrugged. 'The mystery of movie making I guess. Anyway, I've seen all I need to, so we can go now.' Nic turned around, stepped back outside and held the door for Rose.

They drove back to Pinnaroo.

It was around noon when they arrived at the BP Service Station. 'My spies have mentioned I should be vigilant around this time, and it also aligns with the border staff being on a lunch break.'

They ate the yeast buns for lunch, but as nothing was happening, continued to wait. Nic stepped from the car. 'Sorry Rose, I have to well, go and see a man about a horse, you know um, spend a penny, that sort of thing. The Men's toilet in the BP is out of order, so I'll go across the road to the APEX park. I'll be no longer than ten minutes. Please don't hit anyone over the head with a laptop.'

Rose sighed. 'OK, I think I will go inside and get a drink, something to wash down the yeast bun.'

Rose watched Nic cross the road, and then she stepped from the car and entered the service station. There was only one other man inside apart from the console operator. Rose selected a drink and went up to pay.

The man that she had seen before had disappeared somewhere, so she thought nothing of it, then saw a rushing movement in the round mirror above her head- the man had donned a full-faced balaclava and was holding something in front of him. It was long, pointy and covered by a windbreaker. The console operator called out 'Gun, gun' and he ducked down behind his desk.

Rose felt a strong arm around her waist and the man uttered. 'Come on little lady, you're coming with me.' She was dragged backwards and together entered the cooler room between the walls of fridges. They both sat down.

'I saw you at the cricket game, and what's your friend out there doing, and why is he looking at my truck?'

'I don't know. I don't know anything.'

'Who is he? And who are you? I know you're not from around here. Don't mess with me. I've got a gun.'

Rose sighed. 'My name is Rose, and I live in Brisbane. My friend and I are in Pinnaroo looking at stuff. That's what he does, he looks at stuff. He also buys stuff, sells stuff and does stuff. Have you got stuff in your truck? Maybe he wants to look at it.'

The man stood up and watched as Nic slunk his way across the yard, and he was slowly pulling back the front glass door. The man sat back down again moving his jaw from side to side, considering his next play.

'I'm sorry, Mr Um, what can I call you? Do you have a name too?'

'Wade, call me Wade.'

Rose sighed. 'OK, Wade. Do you mind if I grab a drink and some chocolate? Maybe an ice cream too? That's all I came in here for. When in doubt, I go to chocolate.'

'OK, but no sudden movements. I'm trying to think.'

Rose stood up and saw Nic was now inside the service station. He had convinced the console operator to move out from his alcove and let him out the front door.

'So what's your friend's name, Rose? He's not with the police is he?'

'No. His name's Nic Thorn and he is from Ouyen.'

'No way. Not *the* Nic Thorn. Crap.'

'Do you know him?' Wade sighed. 'I certainly do, and I live next door to his sister.' Wade stood up, pulled off the balaclava, peered through the glass and sat down again. 'That's Nic all right. I went to primary school with him. Have always wondered what he was up to now. Are you two like, together or something? How long have you known him?'

Rose took a breath. 'What's the date today, Wade?'

'The sixteenth I think. Why?'

'Well, that makes it about a couple of weeks.'

A voice called out breaking the silence. 'Hey Rose, are you all right in there?'

'Yes Nic, but I'm a bit cold though. Wade says hello too, and says it's been a while. He told me that you two were in jodhpurs together at primary school. He does have a gun though.'

'No, he doesn't, unless he bought another one with him, and managed to walk in there without anyone noticing. His gun is still in the stocks at the back of the truck, and from what I have been told, it is welded in place.'

'Do you have a gun on me, Wade?'

'Not exactly.' Wade pulled back on the coat revealing a broken broom handle and a banister brush, attached with sticky tape.

'Hey, that's a good job, Wade. I mean you only disappeared for a couple of minutes, then popped back up again with the pretend bang, bang.' Rose stood up and then helped Wade up. 'We're coming out Nic. You're right, it is not a gun. It might do for sweeping up the place, but that's about it.'

They both stepped out and Nic walked up to them. 'Hello Wade. It's been a long time, and mate, this recycling thing can't keep going on. It's a little bit illegal.'

'Yeah, I know. It started small, and all the money goes back into the club so I can keep the water up to the grass. I tried to convince Baggy it was the right thing to do, but he quit over it. Left me running it all. I fill Dad's truck with bottles and cans and drive to Adelaide every couple of weeks to claim the cash refund. I guess I got greedy. How did you know? Did your sister give me up?'

'No, it was Baggy Green. He told me all about it at the hospital. I went to your farm to check on the truck while you two were visiting him in Lameroo. It turned out that every time you came back from Adelaide with the truck, there would be a deposit of cash into the Cricket Club's Bank account a day or two later. One of the tellers at the bank submitted a Suspicious Transaction Form, and the EPA called me in to have a look.'

'I shouldn't have told her where I was getting the money from.'

'Well, you shouldn't have asked Baggy Green to help you put in the sprinkler system either.'

Wade sighed. 'Are you going to arrest me or something?'

Rose piped up. 'He's not a cop, Wade.'

Wade nodded. 'At least I can pay for your drink

and chocolate then.' Rose nodded. 'Thanks for the offer. Just leave the money on the console desk, along with some for the broken broom and banister brush too. County folk are a trusting bunch, so it won't go anywhere.'

Wade and Nic went outside and sat in the truck. Nic made a call to the EPA and they agreed to downgrade the fine to a hundred dollars given all funds were going back into the Cricket Club. The contents of the truck were to be transported back to Wade's farm and destroyed. Wade shook his hand on the deal.

'But, what about Damon, the console guy? I mean I was armed with a broomstick gun.'

Nic nodded. 'All sorted. I told Damon it was all a misunderstanding, and you had a cold, that's why you pulled on the silly hat and it covered your face.'

Wade and Nic drove in the truck back to his farm, and they were shovelling the last of the cans and bottles from the truck when Wade finally realised he was losing the income. He stopped shovelling. 'Nic, the club needs the money. It's hard running a club just on memberships alone and we don't make much on the bar tab. The players are no longer hanging around for a drink after a game.'

Nic nodded. 'All sorted, I'll make a call to some people I know from the Gaming Commission - your club may just qualify for an annual government grant.'

Meanwhile, Rose had followed them in the car, and

as they got closer she realised it was an opportunity to meet Nic's elusive sister. The truck had slowed down for the turn and Rose realised it was a double driveway. The truck went to the right, so she went to the left. Rose pressed a little firmer on the accelerator pedal, saw another farmhouse, then pulled the car to a dusty stop, and stepped out. A young woman, who was hanging out the washing came over, she looked mid-30s. They came together at the front gate.

'Hello, I am Rose, and you are?'

'Julie.'

'Nice to meet you finally, Julie.'

'Do I know you?'

'No, but you are Nic Thorn's sister, aren't you?'

'No, I'm Wade's wife, Julie Wilson.'

'I must have the wrong house sorry. Nic and Wade have taken the truck back next door into Nic's sister's place then.'

'No, that's Wade's mother's place. He lost his Dad about five years ago. Wade stores all the farm machinery in the sheds.' Rose considered her next question. 'Do you know any of the other neighbours?'

'No, we only got married a couple of months ago. I used to live in Port Fairy, and haven't had time to meet anyone yet.'

'Damn you, Nic Thorn. Damn, Damn.'

'What's that Rose?'

'Nothing, Julie.'

A car was coming down the drive towards them. It

stopped out the front, and an older woman stepped out of one side. Nic stepped out of the other. Julie waved and looked over to Rose. 'That's Wade's mum.'

Rose approached her quickly. 'Hello, Mrs. Wilson Snr. My name is Rose Palmer, nice to meet you.' The woman smiled. 'Oh, Nic's +1,' but before Rose had an opportunity to ask her about his sister, Mrs Wilson Snr was back in the car, and had headed off.

Rose sighed, then looked at Nic. 'Missed her by that much. Anyway, what's Wade going to do at the club now? The money would've helped meet the water charges.'

Nic nodded. "Well, I've just been advised the club has qualified for an Annual Gaming Grant, and in the meantime, I arranged a five grand deposit into the club's Bank Account to help cover the cost.'

Rose smiled, and then they stepped back into their car and headed back to Adelaide for the flight home to Brisbane.

During the flight, Rose put down the Inflight magazine and looked at Nic. 'Hey, I know what I am going to do with my life now. I am going to write.'

Nic looked at Rose. 'Oh, yes? How to Divorce Your Parents in one easy lesson? An L. Ron Hubbard epic on the theory of everything?'

Rose smiled. 'Nope. It's chick-lit. It's a series about a secret agent man, and his two beautiful femme fatale associates.'

Nic nodded. 'Auto-biographical?'

'Now, if I told you that I would have to kill off the characters in my book in the first chapter, wouldn't I?'

They landed in Brisbane, collected their luggage, made their way to the taxi rank and shared a cab to West End. Sandy and Dog came out to meet them. Nic said his goodbyes and was about to get back into the taxi but he called Rose over:

'Is everything still good, Rose?'

'Yes, I guess.'

'Well, I have something really important to ask you.'

'Oh, yes Nic. What is it this time?'

'Would you be my bride?'

-

<u>*Dedication*</u>

Thanks to John, Paul, George and Ringo for provid-ing the words of my generation.
(Rose, that was The Who, not the Beatles)
(No Nic, they were the Beatles, have you heard of them?)

Keep reading for an excerpt from the next adventures of Nic Thorn and his Associates in 'Two Hurtled Gloves'

<u>Two hurtled Gloves</u>

Rosemary Palmer was standing on a large wrap-around balcony of a holiday apartment at the Sea Temple Resort, Port Douglas, Far North Queensland. The beautiful Four Mile Beach stretched out below her, and yachts with full billowed sails were plying the crystal blue water of the bay, but she was not interested in any of it as she was here to get married. Again.

The last time she stood at the altar, she was to marry a short, fat, and shallow man named Michael because her father needed to secure one of his business deals, and as a nineteen-year-old, she was the sacrificial lamb. The deal fell over in a week, and the marriage lasted less than that.

Rose still remembers the endless arguments with her father: 'I'm still so young, and at uni, Father for God's sake. I can't love him. I don't even like him. Can't you offer up a couple of your luxury cars instead? Please.' Her parents put it down to pre-wedding jitters, but Rose wanted to put herself down with a handful of sleeping tablets and a large glug of Glen Fiddich. The marriage ceremony went through, and she had still not forgiven them some ten years later.

Rose took a deep breath, considered that she had no choice but to go through with it, and called out to Sandy, her BFF, and bridesmaid. 'Sandy, can we go for a walk, please? Can't I at least enjoy my last moments of singledom looking at something beautiful?'

They went to the beach and were amused by all the warning signs: 'Caution – Danger – Stingers, Sharks & Crocodiles are in the water.' Rose looked at Sandy.

'So maybe today isn't the day I go for a swim.'

For further reading from the Nic Thorn and Associates series of scam-busting investigations search for these titles:

Two hurtled Gloves

Welcome back to Nic's world of diversions and distractions, which begins on a golden beach in Port Douglas, tracks down to Tasmania, and up to the banks of Brisbane. Nic has to investigate a wedded miss, the misguided pretence of Tiger tracking, and some banking blasphemy. Rose was to be a bride again, but this time, it didn't exactly go off without a hitch, either. Then, they move on to another tale, this one tracking down the elusive and believed to be extinct Thylacine. Sandy loses her identity, and Nic introduces them to the benign world of banking, but there is much more involved when the loan arranger is unmasked as a fraud.

Three French Bens

Nic's friend, Benoit Trudeau, is one-third of the 'Three French Bens' at the New Crowd Casino in Melbourne. He has just bought into a high-end restaurant, so he calls Nic's Team in to have a look, as the numbers look fishy, and they might have to go angling for the truth. Nic and his crew then head to Rockhampton to help the Queensland Department of Agriculture look into some cattle duffing, as apparently, it's heard a lot up that way. Finally, Sandy has to deal with an old school friend or is that a fiend that has been taking a loan from her, at her expense?

Four brooding Birds

The Australian Department of Agriculture often deals with sneaks and adders, and this time, Nic and the team are brought in to investigate reptile smuggling. Lizards have been discovered stuffed into a women's singlet, and her accomplice is caught with his jocks of frogs, but of course, he denies any knowledge of how they got in there. Then the team tries to drink from the sweet success of wines, but this just turns out to be someone who can't stop whining about how he has to keep everything bottled up inside. To complete another investigation, they have to look into genuine budgie smugglers. Spare the thought.

Five mouldy Bins

This is the 5th novel in the Nic Thorn Caper series. It's Christmas in July, and the Department of Health in Brisbane is concerned that someone may be stuffing their mattress with ill-gotten gains, so Nic and the team bring it to a head – reindeer style. Meanwhile, Sandy and Rose meet up with their 'friend' Dimond, who keeps handing over her hard-earned money (she tells them that anyway) to lease a new rental property for her husband and family as it turns out the Real Estate Agent knows how to manage to take the deposit too, but only ever in cash.

The team gets involved in a diamond scam. The resolution could be clear cut, but getting stranded in Dubai on the way to South Africa was never in the plan.

Six Geezers Lying

This time, they are brought in for a crash course into a car crashing. Car insurance companies are being driven up the wall by bogus claims and 'accidents', so it's time someone gives the scammers a crash course on how to stop. Then, one of the national restaurant chains puts together a competition that anyone can win, but what happens when the prizes are won even before the competition is finished? Is it a competition if there are only winners? Then Rose finds out her Father is running an art show, but she thinks he is just being scammed. Art is not always art, as it depends on your point of view, but fraud is always a fraud.

Seven Hapless Hoops

Organisations keep looking to Nic Thorn and his Associates to sort stuff out. A person is missing, a car is missing, and it's a lot of horsing around for Nic and his team. This time, one of his old school friends calls upon him to locate his missing wife; whilst this is not generally within the scope of what they do, it is too close to home for Nic not to be in the right place to investigate. Meantime, a car vanishes without a trace, and a horse race is gathering pace, but will they be too late to save face?

AUTHOR'S BIOGRAPHY

The author is a former long-term banker by profession and worked within the Bank's Credit Card Fraud Team, where he obtained a Private Investigators License. The author resides between Adelaide, South Australia, and the Sunshine Coast, Queensland. He has been fortunate to have visited many places in Australia and includes them in these stories.

In November 2022, the author won an award from Wakefield Press, Adelaide for his short story: 'Car on a Hill'.

Other published titles: 'The Flighters – Believe.'

www.ingramcontent.com/pod-product-compliance
Lightning Source LLC
Chambersburg PA
CBHW070014120726
47909CB00003B/928